MW00880822

Published by Jan Stryvant

#59327Ba
ISBN-13: 978-1979799492
ISBN-10: 1979799490

Jan Stryvant Books:

The Valens Legacy
- Black Friday   Book 1
- Perfect Strangers Book 2
- Over Our Heads   Book 3
- Head Down   Book 4
- When It Falls   Book 5

Shadow

Saturday

Sean was standing at the counter at the McDonalds on North Virginia, just across the street from the casino. It was a little after two, and he'd been woken up by his hunger. Neither of the girls was there, and he was hesitant to use his phone. So he decided to go out and get some food, before he passed out or something. Apparently using magic burned up a lot of calories.

Besides, it was Saturday, and being spring break, Reno was packed with college kids looking to have a little fun. With that kind of crowd, he was sure he'd be able to lose himself easily enough.

He had ducked into the Silver Legacy on the way there, figuring on using its wards to throw off anyone who just might be looking for him. Then he'd run across the street, made his order, paid, and he figured he'd be back into the warded area within five minutes, ten minutes tops.

The guy at the counter had just finished handing him the rather large bag with all of his burgers in it, when his eyes got wide and Sean just instinctively dodged left as the guy silently crumpled to the floor.

Sean cut a hard right next, running through the dinning area and then dropping his shoulder he just rammed the door to the kitchen hard, breaking it open and turning left again, he ran for the back door.

He could hear footsteps pounding behind him, there were people giving chase, how many, he had no idea.

Hitting the back door and coming out into the alley, he turned to the south and started to run as hard as he could, the bag with the burgers still held in a tight grip in his left hand.

He'd kill them before he gave up his damn lunch!

Glancing back behind him as he cut around the back of the Thunderbird, Sean saw four men in pretty typical outfits chasing him: Slacks, light jackets that were open and flapping in the breeze, exposing some rather strange looking holsters. Wands?

They were all probably early twenties, and they were already panting hard. Definitely *not* the physical fitness types Sean guessed.

Checking the traffic Sean cut across Fourth Street, horns blaring at him as he dodged right through the traffic, vaulting a car hood. Slowing down a moment, he grabbed a burger out of the bag, and peeling the wrapper he dropped it and started to eat as he picked up speed again, going south down Virginia, dodging in and out of people.

Halfway down the block, he stopped and looked behind him. Two more had joined the chase; a car was trying to make a u-turn in the traffic back in front of the McDonalds, one of the doors swinging closed as the drivers of the other cars signaled their displeasure at the idiot making a u-turn in traffic.

Turning back to run south again, Sean finished his burger quickly, then pulled out another one and tossing that wrapper on the ground Sean then cut a sudden right, dodging through traffic again on Virginia, cutting in front of a bus, and giving the driver a heart attack he was sure.

Sean slowed down a bit; he wanted to be sure they saw him and followed. It was time to teach yet another harsh lesson to these people. Glancing back, he saw one suddenly point as they were milling around looking for him, and they all took off again after him.

Smiling, Sean picked up speed, sprinting across Sierra Street with no honking horns but several cars locked their brakes, screeching to a stop. It was time to put all of that hard-earned local knowledge to use. When he got to West, he crossed that too and then very visibly jumped up and grabbing the chain link fence by the railroad tracks, he flipped over the top, and quickly climbed back down.

As soon as he was out of sight, he dropped the twenty feet down to the tracks below. Unwrapping another burger, he dropped the wrapper for that one in plain sight between the tracks and then slowly jogged back east, into the tunnel that the train went through in the center of town. There were access ways down here, and one of them led up into the El Dorado casino. When Sean had bussed tables at the buffet there as a high school student, he'd learned about them when the other bus boys wanted to go hide from the bosses and get stoned on their breaks.

Sean wondered if scrying spells worked through dirt? There was quite a bit above him now, he'd have to ask Jolene about that. He'd also have to do something about this whole scrying thing. Hopefully there was a spell in one of those books someplace he could use.

Stopping near the metal access door he needed, Sean slipped his shoes off, unbuttoned the first few buttons on his shirt and shrugged out his vest. Shifting, he popped the rest of the burger he'd been eating into his muzzle and then grabbed the door handle with one hand while placing the other on the wall next to it and with a soft growl he slowly exerted pressure and pulled it open, the locking bar creaking loudly as it bent and then gave way, allowing the door to swing open.

Pulling out another burger, Sean made sure the wrapper for this one went back into the bag, and then he hunkered down, lying prone next to the tracks to see just what they'd do.

Sean didn't have long to wait, two of the ones that had followed him out of the back of the McDonald's floated down, landing rather clumsily by the discarded wrapper.

"He went in there! Go block off the other side!" one of them said into his phone, while the other one peered into the darkness.

"Now what?" the other one asked softly. Sean thanked his lycan hearing, they might as well have been yelling, considering just how quiet it was down here.

"We go in and get him. He's just a kid, what's he gonna do? Hell, after that drop I'd be surprised if his legs aren't broken."

"Then why didn't the Lithos get him?"

"Because he had a guardian, that's why. But the Lithos killed him," the other one muttered as they started forward. "I don't know why the hell you're so scared, no one's gonna care what happens to him. The kid's a wimp, a video gamer."

"I don't know, he sure ran pretty fast."

"And kept slowing down while stuffing his face," the other man laughed.

Sean eased his pistol out and sighted on the one with the phone.

"You guys there.... Damn, lost my signal."

"Maybe we should wait until they cover the other end?"

"Dammit, Johnson. Do you want to face Harkins and the rest and tell them we let some mundane kid get away? Now shut up!"

"Then why hasn't anyone else gotten him?"

"Because up until now, no one else has tried, obviously. Do you really think this kid is smarter than we are? He was in a fucking McDonalds! Really now...."

Sean pulled the trigger, and hit the guy in the chest; the look of shock on his face only lasted a moment as Sean shot him a second time and then switched to Johnson who had jumped at the loud roar of the gun in the enclosed tunnel. Sean shot him twice too, and then turned to look the other way as both men dropped to the ground, very dead.

Sean grumbled and wished for ear plugs as his ears rang, but interestingly enough the ringing quickly subsided, and a minute later he watched two men drop down at the other end of the tunnel, three hundred yards away.

Sean waited patiently and ate two more burgers as the men approached. These two were a bit more wary than the other two had been, and both of them had something in their hands. What they were holding, Sean couldn't tell for sure, but they obviously weren't pistols of any sort.

"I don't see anyone," one of the two hissed softly as they got closer, "cast a light spell, we should be able to see Johnson's and Simms' outlines by now!"

"We can't use magic! What if someone sees us doing it? They probably followed the kid through an access way or something."

"We're in a tunnel, smartass; no one is going to see anything."

"Oh, yeah," he said, and as Sean watched he put whatever it was he was carrying back into his holster and then raised his hands and made a gesture. Realizing that he was about to be exposed, Sean shot the one who wasn't casting first, and then immediately shot the other one as light suddenly blazed into the tunnel.

Swearing at the suddenly brightness, Sean closed his eyes, trying to hunker down as close to the ground as he could. When the ringing in his ears stopped, he opened his eyes and looked down the now well-lit tunnel. Sean could see that he'd only wounded the second one, the one that had cast the spell, and who was now trying to crawl back they way they'd come.

Shifting back into his human form, Sean set the bag of food down and carefully started walking towards the man, gun pointed at him as he did.

"You murdered my father," Sean said, and the man suddenly rolled over and tried to draw what looked like a taser from the odd holster under his jacket. Sean quickly stepped on the man's arm, pinning it to the ground before he could get his weapon out.

"You killed my best friend," Sean growled down at him.

"That wasn't us! That was somebody else!" the man said, eyes locked on the gun in Sean's hand.

"You kidnapped my mother, probably killed her too," Sean's voice got louder and his hand tightened on the pistol's grip

"No! That wasn't us! We didn't do that!"

"And you were going to kill me too, weren't you?" Sean said, staring down the sights of his pistol as he aimed it at the man's head, thinking about all those people that had died yesterday. About what had been done to his family. About what they were going to do to him the moment that they got their hands on him.

Sean started to snarl as the anger rose up inside him.

The man's eyes got wide and his left hand rose, "Ra...."

Sean shot him in the head. Three times. He would have shot him four, but the slide had locked open.

Changing magazines, Sean re-holstered his pistol, picked up his brass, and looked at what he'd done. Sean hadn't let his lion pull the trigger on this one, oh no, this time he'd pulled the trigger himself.

Shaking his head he took their weapons, went and got the weapons from the other two, which also looked to be some sort of taser like device, probably magical. Then he went back to the door and picked up the remaining six expelled cartridges and put them all in his pocket. Putting his shoes back on and picking up his bag of food, he used his vest to grab the handle of the door and pulling it open, he went inside.

There were at least three more of these guys looking for him, but Sean doubted that they knew the back corridors and the basement halls like he did.

It took Sean a good ten minutes to make his way back up into the casino proper, and he made sure to dodge the security cameras that were along the route. Another thing he'd learned from the other busboys. Not like security was all that concerned with the goings on of the maintenance staff or the cooks, the crimes they were worried about took place out on the gaming floor or in the cashier's booths.

Ducking into one of the employee bathrooms, he locked himself in one of the stalls and took the time to finish off his lunch. He was still hungry and they couldn't scry him in here, so why rush?

Once he'd finished eating, Sean crumbled the bag up and tossed it and the dead men's weapons into one of the trashcans and then took a long drink of water from one of the faucets. There were three more guys, if they were still looking for him. He had seen two of them. He'd have to keep his eyes open and move carefully.

Leaving the bathroom, he moved down the hall to one of the entrances that led back to one of the public hallways. After peeking out the door and making sure that no one in it looked like they were looking for anybody, Sean slipped out and joined the crowd.

Moving down the hallway, he stopped when he got to the transition from one casino to the next, and peeked quickly around the corner.

There was someone standing there, watching the people going by, and he looked a lot like one of the two from the car.

Stepping back, Sean retraced his steps. There was a gift shop, the areas between the casinos were full of them, stepping inside he saw a rack of sweatshirts. Grabbing one that said 'Go Pack' and had a wolf's head on it he quickly paid for it and left the store.

Once outside he stuck his vest in the bag they'd given him, and put the sweatshirt on. He'd grabbed one way too big for him, but right now that worked out well, the gun under his shirt would definitely draw unwanted attention without his vest on.

Moving back up to the corner, Sean waited for a large gaggle of people, once he got past the transition area, which actually was a wide archway over the street below that had been stuffed with slot machines, Sean could duck back into a service corridor.

Spying a group of drunken college kids, Sean slipped into the middle of them, slouching down as they walked past the guy keeping an eye out for him. But as they passed, Sean noticed that there were two other people there now, people he didn't recognize, and they were arguing with the first man.

What they were saying, Sean couldn't hear over the noise, but he'd seen enough turf fights to know one when he saw one, and the nearby security guard made it clear that security had seen it too.

This was rather curious. Were they from another organization? Or was this an internal disagreement?

Leaving the group who had suddenly noticed their new member, Sean ducked back down into a service corridor and decided that right now, he didn't want to know.

Consequences

Sean sighed and climbed the stairs, two flights a floor, back and forth, as he thought about what had just happened. His world had truly gone to hell, utter and complete hell. Just setting foot outside, anywhere, was a deadly risk. He wondered about the poor guy back at that counter, was he dead? Was he okay?

Sean shook his head, and then there were those four guys he'd just killed. Oh, he didn't doubt that they deserved it; they intended the same for him he was sure. Like it or not, this was a war now. They weren't going to go away; they weren't going to leave him alone. The only way out of this was to win it.

Now if only he knew just what the hell he was fighting for.

Coming out of the stairwell onto the top floor, he found both Roxy and Jolene were waiting for him. The relief on both of their faces was obvious as they rushed over and hugged him.

"Where were you?" Jolene asked.

"And why does your gun smell like you've been shooting it?" Roxy growled, looking a cross between worried and angry.

"I got hungry, so I went to McDonalds," Sean said guiltily while blushing.

"You went to McDonalds and had lunch?" Roxy said giving him a rather dark look.

"Well, originally I was just going to pop in, get the food, and bring it back here. I figured I'd be outside of the casino wards for a few minutes at the most, but there was a umm," Sean sighed, "I got jumped at McDonalds and had to make a run for it."

"What!" Roxy said, shocked. Even Jolene looked surprised.

Sean nodded, "I guess they have the area staked out or something. I don't think I was in there five minutes before they were on me."

"How could you do something so idiotic? Tell me what happened!" Roxy demanded.

Sean stood up straight and looked down at Roxy, "I was starving. No one was here and you didn't leave a note."

Roxy opened her mouth, and then suddenly realized that a cheetah trying to chew out a lion probably wasn't the smartest move for the cheetah. Even if the lion loved said cheetah.

"I'm sorry, Sean. But you scared me. A lot. I was afraid something bad had happened to you."

Sean nodded and gave Roxy a hug. Sure, he realized *now* that yes, it was an idiotic thing to do. So why had he gotten so offended?

'Hey, I thought I told you no growling at our Roxy?'

'We didn't growl' the thought came back, *'and if we don't maintain our dominance, she won't respect us.'*

"I didn't think they'd be on me so fast," Sean sighed and wondered if maybe his lion had a point, Roxy hadn't pulled back from him, in fact she was leaning into him maybe a little harder now. "Obviously I made a small mistake."

"Where are they now?" Jolene asked.

"I ambushed four of them," Sean said, suddenly feeling a little embarrassed.

"That doesn't sound good," Roxy said looking up at him.

"Well, for them it wasn't," Sean agreed and told them what happened. He tried to recall as much as possible about what he'd heard them say, and remembered to mention his question about scrying people underground.

"The one thing I can't figure out," Sean said, after he'd finished, "is why they keep trying to engage me in small groups. They keep acting like I'm some dumb kid, even after everything that's happened to the ones sent after me so far."

"Oh, that's easy to explain," Jolene said. "You have to understand that these are all competing groups. They don't share intelligence on anything important. They're not going to tell any of their rivals about how they tried to grab you and failed spectacularly.

"Also, it's like what you heard the one guy say, they thought your friend killed the first group, and I doubt that the Vestibulum or Gradatim have told anyone, even most of their own members, about what you did to them."

"So, those two I saw arguing with the one guy?"

"Yeah, they were probably arguing over who was going to get you. Remember, some of these groups want you dead, some just want to get their hands on you to take what they think you have."

"Aren't there any groups out there who don't want to get involved?" Sean grumbled.

"Probably," Jolene shrugged, "but I have no idea who they are yet. I think a lot of people are still laying low after yesterday's elemental attack; that was a pretty major event for a small city like Reno.

"But right now, there is one thing I can tell you."

"And that is?"

"Don't set foot outside of this building until you have learned how to keep anyone from scrying your location. Oh, and yes, being underground will block scrying. But it has to be under *ground*, beneath the dirt. Concrete won't do it; something about the things living in the earth and on top of the soil blocks it."

Sean nodded, "So, where were you two?"

"Jolene went out to talk to her friends in the magical community," Roxy said. "While I was out getting food," and she pointed to two large shopping bags. "I thought I'd be back *before* you woke up."

Sean snorted and gave Roxy a kiss on the forehead, "Okay, my bad. Now how about we eat and Jolene can tell us what she learned?" Sean gave Roxy a pat on the butt and let go of both of the girls.

"I thought you just ate?" Roxy asked, but Sean could tell she was teasing.

"And what kind of lion would I be if I didn't eat my mate's food when she brought it back for me?" He teased back. From the way her hips twitched as she walked over to the bags, Sean realized that he'd definitely said the right thing. Apparently she liked getting him food, probably just another one of those lycan things he would learn about with time.

"And what did you learn?" Sean asked Jolene, turning to look at her as went and sat down at the table they'd been using.

"Nothing good, I'm afraid," Jolene sighed. "It wasn't ten dead from the elemental attack; it looks like now that it was more than twenty people who were killed."

"Twenty?" Sean joined her at the table and sat down. "Why so many?"

"Well, it turns out that there were a lot more petty scores being settled than any of us realized. Then it looks like that there were five people, not just one, who were in the wrong place at the wrong time."

"Innocent victims?"

Jolene nodded, "That's what people are thinking."

Sean shook his head and growled, "I don't care so much about the mages killing each other, but the others? Killing people because they're in the wrong place at the wrong time? Or because they *might* become allies of mine, if, *if*, just maybe, just possibly, I might have been left something by my father? Something I just *might* be able to use?

"*If* they'd just left this all alone, I wouldn't even know what was going on! Even *if* I had learned about it, the odds of me actually doing anything about it were zero! I was happy with my life! I wasn't looking to change the world."

Sean just put his head in his hands and stared down at the table. "All of these people dead because of me. Hell! I've killed how many of them now myself?"

He felt Roxy's hand start stroking down his back, comforting him, "It's not your fault, Hon. They did this. They started it; they caused it; they never gave you any choice."

Jolene reached across the table and put her hand over his as well.

"She's right, Hon. Too many of them view themselves as above the law, as above the regular mundane people that surround them. Yes, we're different; yes some of us have powers that others don't. But that doesn't give us, or them, the right to kill or abuse others.

"Sadly, however, this has been going on for far too long."

"Well, I guess it's going to be up to me to try and change it," Sean said looking up at Jolene. "So, what else did you learn?"

"Well, everyone is pretty uneasy right now, and there are a lot of eyes on Reno, which means you too, Sean. Rumors are beginning to spread in the magical community about you, as well as the supernatural ones. No one is really sure what to believe; even the seers are saying things are too confused to know what's going to happen anymore."

"So," Roxy said, "right now the best thing to do is just to hunker down and come Monday we'll go see just what's in that safety deposit box."

"And after that?" Sean asked.

"I guess we wait and see what happens on your birthday."

Sean snorted, "And here I was just planning on going out and getting legally drunk that day."

"Well," Jolene said and reaching into her handbag she pulled out a couple of candles, "as long as you've got nothing to do, how about practicing?"

"You're a slave driver, you know that?" Sean grinned.

"Maybe if you're nice I'll show you all my whips and chains," Jolene teased in a husky voice.

Sean rolled his eyes while Roxy laughed and started setting food on the table.

"Food first, then you can work on lighting candles."

Jolene nodded, "After you eat, I have a new spell I want you to learn."

"Oh? What is it?" Sean asked.

"One to blow out candles, of course!"

It was dark when Sean finally ran out of candles. There were twelve melted piles of wax on the table; he'd spent all day lighting and blowing out each of them, one after the other, for hours. The spell that Jolene had taught him wasn't that hard, but learning it! *That* was a tough lesson. Jolene's approach to magic was different than the one in his books, and with it he gained a lot more insight on how to do it all.

Now he had all of these thoughts, these spell fragments, as he thought about the two spells he now knew, floating around in his head. He spent some time pulling them apart in his head and trying to get the big picture. Trying to understand how it all worked.

The problem was, he needed to learn some more spells, but not right now. Right now he needed to stretch his legs and walk around for a while. He needed to get some exercise, and while he couldn't go out, he had twenty floors plus a basement and a sub-basement he could explore.

Going over to where Roxy and Jolene were sleeping, Sean woke Roxy up.

"Hmmm? What?" Roxy asked, sleepily.

"I'm going to explore the building, want to come?"

"No, just don't go outside," Roxy yawned and closing her eyes, she rolled over and went back to sleep.

Sean smiled down at the two of them and briefly entertained the idea of waking them both up for some other kinds of fun, but he could feel his lion's urge to explore his current territory.

So stripping off his shirt and pants, Sean shifted into his lion form, and then padded down the stairs to the ground floor to begin his explorations.

There were a lot of exits from the ground floor of course, and all of the ones going directly outside had been boarded up some years ago. There were a few doors to the other tower, but all of those were locked.

The basement was interesting, but it was primarily storage and what looked like a couple of now empty offices for building staff. Sean did find where the electrical power came into the building, as well as the phone and data lines. Each of those spots had an access way, which led out of the building and into an underground vault, that Sean could tell was under the street outside of the building. The overhead tube leading up to a manhole cover gave that away.

The cableways leading out of the chamber and down the streets were of course far too narrow for anyone to go through.

The sub-basement was mostly dank and dark and had a much lower ceiling. It was taken up with a lot of waste pipes, and a couple of machines rooms that Sean really had no idea what they were for. He did however find the access to the sewers. It was actually fairly large, and peeking inside, Sean suspected that you could probably travel a fair distance by them, if you wanted to.

But the stench of it quickly dissuaded any idea of going inside and looking around. Hastily closing the door Sean decided it was time to go back upstairs and go to bed, he could check out some of the other floors tomorrow.

Sunday

"Hi, Hon. How goes it?" Roxy said coming up behind him with a large bag of food as he concentrated on evaporating another drop of water. Sean had learned three new spells in his 'classroom' this morning. The first created a drop of water from the moisture in the air. The second froze it into a small bead of ice. The third heated it up, first melting it, and then turning it into steam. Those were the only other spells in the 'Learning to Cast' book.

"Slow, but steady," Sean sighed getting up and wobbling a little, "And surprisingly tiring," he grinned lopsidedly and hugged Roxy, and then kissed her.

"And hungry, very, very, hungry!" he growled as she handed him the grocery bag. There were a dozen quarter-pounder's on the top and he started in on those with a will, sitting down on one of the couches.

"What's it like out there?" Sean asked between bites.

"People are *still* talking about 'the storm,'" she said making quote marks with her fingers. "A lot of the people who got struck by lighting have finally made the news, as well as the fire at the college, *and* the suspicious explosions at a trailer park."

Sean sighed and shook his head, "Has my name come up in any of this?"

"No, but I think it's only a matter of time until some bright boy puts it together, or someone in the police department leaks it to the news media."

"How bad was the damage at our apartments? Did the house burn down?"

"I called Cindy, one of my friends on the first floor. She told me that it looks like the top floor got it pretty bad, but everyone else's rooms only got some water damage and the house has been temporarily condemned until they clean it up."

Sean shook his head, "Let me guess, it started in my room?"

"Actually, no, it started in George's room."

"Shit! How is he?"

"Fine I gather. Cindy told me that he told the police that his stereo just suddenly burst into flames while he was doing his homework. So the fire department thinks there was a power surge or something."

"I'm surprised it wasn't in my room," Sean shook his head.

"I don't think they were trying to kill you, just grab you. Remember, there were people watching outside when I ran out of the building, watching us."

Sean nodded, "I guess we just have to wait and see what Jolene tells us when she gets back. You want any of these?" Sean asked, offering one of the burgers to Roxy.

"Thanks, Hon," Roxy said smiling, and taking it she sat down next to him.

Sean noticed she was all but purring and had scooted over to press her leg against his.

"How did I just make you so happy?" Sean asked, grinning.

"When a male shares his food with a female, *especially* when he's starving, it shows everyone that he's in love."

"Well, yeah, I'm in love," Sean chuckled. "So, is that one from your psych class?"

"Nope," Roxy grinned, "it's a lycan thing. Well, at least with us predators."

Sean shook his head, "You're not hungry, are you?"

"Nope!" Roxy laughed, "I ate while getting you food. But there's no *way* I'm turning this burger down!"

Sean put an arm around her and gave her a hug. "As long as you're happy, I'm happy."

"So what kind of spells are you casting?" Roxy asked, and then grinned and took a big bite out of her burger.

Sean told her the three spells he was casting over and over at this point.

"They're the last ones in the beginner's book. Once I have those down, I get to move into an intermediate book, with more complicated spells."

"I thought you said it was like computer programming, and you understood it?"

Sean nodded, "I understand the theory completely. But I still have to learn just how to *use* the language of it, the code. The simple spells look simple, but the act of gathering your power, and then shaping it to form those code words," Sean grimaced, "that's a bit harder than I expected.

"And then there's the mnemonics! A lot of wizards use pretty standard ones, and they're in the books. But after something Jolene told me, I'm not so sure that I want to use those."

"Why not? What did she say?"

"She told me that she just makes up a lot of her spells as she goes along."

"You can do that?" Roxy asked and took another bite.

Sean nodded, "Yeah, you can, but it's not easy. Jolene is a lot smarter than she lets on, and after looking over the language, I can see just how it's done. But the mnemonics that everyone seems to use, they're pretty limiting. I don't know if that's intentional, or if they just grew up that way. They're like a fourth generation language in computing."

"So they hide what's really going on from the user," Roxy supplied.

"Exactly so," Sean agreed. "So I'm trying to come up with my own mnemonic gestures and phrases."

Roxy thought about that a moment, "Just what kinds of gestures do you need?"

"Any kind, really. The hard part is that you need to be able to build on them, so as your skill builds you can easily build more complicated gestures. It's the reason that people have spell books and study them, because they forget just what does which as they get more complicated."

"Why not just use ASL?"

"ASL?"

"American sign language," Roxy shrugged her shoulders, "then you don't have to remember anything, you just write out what you're doing."

Raising a finger Sean started to say, "That wouldn't ...." then stopped, shut his mouth, and thought about it a moment.

"They also have complete words for things, not just letters, right?"

Roxy nodded and ate the last bite of her burger.

"Huh, I wonder why nobody else has thought of that?"

Roxy swallowed the last of her burger and got out a bottle of water. "Maybe they have, maybe it's something that only the powerful users know, maybe they give everyone those standard mnemonics to keep them from getting too powerful."

Sean smiled and pulling her close with his arm he hugged her again, then he kissed her after she'd finished taking a drink from her bottle.

"That's an awesome idea! I'm definitely doing it! Now I just need to find someone to teach it to me."

"Oh, that's simple," Roxy said and holding up her right hand she rattled off the alphabet, making each sign as she did.

"You know sign language?" Sean blinked, looking at her as she smirked back at him, and winked.

"One of my friends growing up was mute. If we wanted to know what she was saying, we had to learn it. Of course, once we did that, we all used it to say things to each other when we didn't want anyone else to know what we were talking about!"

"You must have gotten in a lot of trouble," Sean laughed and shook his head.

"Yeah, my mom and dad had to learn it, just to keep me in line. Then of course dad started making his deputies learn it."

"Why'd he do that?"

"So they could talk to each other across a room without shouting, and without letting the bad guys know what they were up to. Not many people know it."

"Well, I hear Jolene coming; we can start on my lessons later."

"Uh-uh, no playing for you," Roxy teased. "You need to keep studying."

"Awww," Sean mock pouted and went back to work.

"You know, one of you could have come down and carried me up," Jolene said, still out of breath when she finally entered the room a few minutes later.

"Maybe we just want you to keep that nice firm ass," Sean teased.

"Why do I even try?" Jolene grumbled.

"Because we love you?" Roxy giggled.

"And because of what we do to you!" Sean added with a grin. "So, what else have you learned today?"

"That it's a good time not to be in Reno," Jolene sighed, dropping down onto the couch next to Roxy. Sean was already sitting on the floor working on his spells again.

"Oh, neat combo there, Sean," Jolene said, looking over his shoulder a moment.

"That bad then?" Sean asked and finished up what he was doing for now.

"There are so many factions right now, that you can't tell them apart without a scorecard. Those folks who set your apartment house on fire?"

"What about them?"

"They were trying to get their hands on you to protect you from the coming storm summoning."

"Riiiiight," Roxy drawled sarcastically.

"They panicked. They knew time was short and so they just ran there and did what they did."

"Does that mean that they're good guys?" Sean asked.

"They're better guys than the ones who just want to kill you outright, or take you home and make you tell them everything. But I don't know if I would call them 'good.' Like I said, they were rushed. If they had gotten you, who knows what it could have devolved into."

"So what are the lycans doing?"

"Keeping their heads down and not saying a word. Best I can guess, and trust me, this is only a guess; most of them are waiting to see what happens after your birthday. No one wants to stick their head up, for fear of getting it cut off, unless they *know* it's worth the risk."

Sean nodded, "Can't say that I blame them."

"Just make sure you stay off the streets, even after you do learn to block their scrying."

"Huh? Why?"

"Because they're all out there, walking around, looking for you. What you did to those four guys from the Harkins' coven? *Everyone* knows about it now. It even made the news last night, and though the mundanes are thinking drug activity, the people looking for you are concentrating on the downtown area now, because this is the last place you were seen before disappearing again.

"You might get away with being outside in the dark, but in the broad daylight? Not a chance. They're really starting to go crazy out there. Thursday's storm has shown a lot of folks just what some people are willing to do, and now you've shown everybody that you're not going to go down without a fight, a lot of folks are worried and are thinking that there just might be something to the rumors of you carrying on your father's work. There's even this whole 'if we can't have him, nobody can' vibe going out there with some of the groups."

"Well how the hell are we going to get to the bank tomorrow then?"

"Are you sure you want to go," Jolene asked.

Sean nodded, "I'm in the dark here, hell, we're all in the dark here. No one really knows what's going on, or if they do, they're not talking. Knowledge is power, right? Well I need to see just what's in there. If it answers just one question, I need to get it."

Jolene nodded, "Okay, give me some time to think about it. We can talk about it later, and make a plan. While I'm at it, you might as well see if there *are* any protection from scrying spells in those books you got in your head."

"There are, they're in a book called 'Hidden Ways.'"

"Good, go study them."

"Now?" Sean looked at her surprised.

Jolene nodded, "Yeah, if you can do that," she motioned to the small wet spot where the ice drop had been, "you can do this."

Sean sighed and nodded. Jolene was right; it was definitely time to see what he could do.

Let the Games Begin

Sean yawned; he was in the back of his mom's car, down on the floor, with a blanket over him. He'd been up until three am, but he'd learned the protection from scrying spell and had been able to cast it. But that wasn't the only thing he'd learned, he'd learned how to cast a spell on himself, and a lot of the meanings of the commands in the language of magic as well as a much better understanding of the syntax. He was starting to see a lot of possibilities for hacking magic now as well.

When he cast the spell, he'd done it the 'slow' way, by building it step by step in his head, as the books had taught him, watching as each piece fell into place. He'd seen several places where things could be done better, and more streamlined, by using the techniques he'd either learned in college, or he'd taught himself from his gaming. So he'd done them and then had Jolene examine the final product.

She'd been rather pleased.

So he got Roxy to teach him a few words in sign language, and then he'd attached the spell to them.

Then he'd cast it on himself again, as well as Roxy and Jolene as practice. Sean was already starting to get the idea for creating some magical language 'libraries' not unlike the ones many programming languages came with. He figured if he could reduce a lot of the standard spells and standard spell structures to single 'reference' he'd be able to skip over a lot of what was in the books, and just create his own spells on the spot.

He'd have to create a few simple spell frameworks of course, but looking over the cost of most spells, even with fifty some-odd points, he wasn't going to get more then twenty or so if he did things the traditional way. And while that might be enough for a typical beginner, Sean didn't have the time for that. He needed to rape the rules like a serious D&D rules lawyer; he needed to go full munchkin.

And he was starting to see some seriously large loopholes that were ripe for abuse using his programming and gaming skills. The only problem was, he was still learning the rules, the basic commands, and how they interacted in the language.

You can't break the rules, or at least bend the hell out of them, until you knew them after all.

"Okay, here we go," Roxy said and they pulled out of the gated parking garage for the smaller north tower where Jolene had her apartment. It was early still, six am. Which was why Sean was so tired. But they all agreed that the sooner they set out and got away from downtown, the safer it would be. There were just too many people looking for him downtown, now that it was the last place he'd been spotted.

So as Sean lay in the back of the car on the floor he played with his spell. It was interesting, because with one of the changes he'd made to it, he could actually feel the spell working. And it was working a *lot*! There were dozens of people trying to scry him, though their attempts were weak, because they were casting over such a large area.

The way the spell avoided them was that it simply just didn't allow their attempts to 'ping' him to get a response. It was a lot like a computer network when you got right down to it. Everyone had an identity that was unique to themselves. So when you wanted to scry for someone, you sent out a request for all the identities in a region, like a computer on a network. Then you applied filters to your responses, again not unlike a computer search, only these filters were based on what you knew about your target that was unique to them.

The scrying spell itself was very costly, because it had to cover a fair amount of territory and sort through a lot of people. Sean could now see why that one guy was driving around in the car: the spell moved with the caster, so a smaller area focus, less energy. Setting up the filters could be costly too, however if you had one or two key aspects to focus on, your filter could be simple, and therefore rather cheap to apply. Then you just weeded through the responses until you found the one that was who you were looking for.

The easiest way to stop someone from pinging you on a network was of course to get off the network. But Sean didn't see a way to do that here. For that matter, it might not even be possibly to be off the 'network' and still be alive.

But there was an easier way to deal with it than the spell's method of blocking requests, and a much cheaper way magically as well. All he had to do was stop 'accepting' any such requests.

Thinking about that, Sean wondered what other aspects of his own self were easily interacted with by outsiders? Either from a distance, or much closer, by touch?

But did he really need to know all of them? A computer didn't need to know everything that might hit one of its ports to be able to block *all* of them with a firewall.

Sean smiled to himself and turned that idea over in his head, a firewall. He could construct a firewall spell that would not allow any contact, any connections, to him at all. He could then add exceptions to it, he was sure, if it turned out there were any connections that he wanted to allow. Just like a firewall on a computer.

Concentrating on his watch he opened up his classroom and started to look through the 'Hidden Ways' spell book. Sean saw the same basic format of the protection from scrying spell he'd used applied over and over again, on those spells that focused on hiding yourself, or aspects about you, from those trying to view them magically or remotely.

It could definitely work.

Feeling himself being shaken, Sean closed the book and exited his classroom.

"You sleeping back there?" Jolene asked.

"Sleeping back there, what?" Sean smirked.

"Sean," Jolene said.

"Try again!"

Jolene rolled her eyes to the ceiling and sighed while smiling. "Hon."

Sean sat up and kissed her, then slid back onto the rear seat. "Better!" he chuckled. "And no, I was actually studying scrying spells and how to hide from them. I think I found a better and cheaper way."

"Oh? And what would that be?"

"Firewalls," Sean said with a smirk. "So, what did you want?"

"We're here," Roxy said, turning the car off.

"That soon?"

"We've been driving around for two hours!" Roxy said looking back at him, now that he was sitting up in the seat. "Don't you have any sense of time while you're studying?"

Sean blushed, "I sorta got caught up in what I was doing. So, um, now what?"

"Let's go get breakfast over there," Roxy said and pointed at a cafe that was just opening up for the day's business. "Then after we eat, we can go hit the bank."

Sean nodded as his stomach growled. "Sounds good to me."

"Do all lycans eat this much?" Jolene asked Roxy.

"He's still filling out. Haven't you noticed the extra muscle on him?"

"Actually no," Jolene said looking back at Sean.

"Well maybe if you weren't forcing me to study so much and gave me some more 'quality time with teacher,' you would?" Sean said with a wink.

"Yeah, really, Jolene," Roxy laughed, "You need to put your hands on him more."

Sean was rather surprised to see Jolene blush.

"I, umm, guess I need to at that," Jolene ducked her head in agreement.

"Come on, let's go eat," Roxy said and getting out of the car nearly dragged them both inside. "You're not the only ones who are hungry!"

They got to the bank just shortly after it opened.

"Hi, I need to check my safety deposit box?" Sean said, coming up to one of the tellers.

"Do you have an account with us?" She asked.

Sean nodded and gave her his name and account number.

"That's strange, Mr. Valens. I don't see you listed as having a box,"

Sean opened his mouth, but Jolene put her hand on his arm.

"It's a confidential one," Jolene said with a smile. "Could we speak to the bank manager, in private please?"

The teller just nodded and smiled, "Of course! Please have a seat while I call him."

"What's that all about?" Sean asked in a whisper as they went over to the seats.

"Just let me deal with him," Jolene smiled.

Sean glanced at Roxy, who just shrugged.

"Sure," he said.

A few minutes later a man came over an introduced himself as the bank manager and led them to a private office.

"So, the teller told me you have a safety deposit box with us?" As he indicated the seats in his office.

"Oh, yes," Jolene said and putting her hand on his arm, she leaned in towards him rather seductively. "I was hoping you could help us?"

Sean noticed that the man's eyes immediately looked down the top of Jolene's open blouse. Sean almost took a step forward, but Roxy put her hand on Sean's arm, stopping him.

"But there aren't any boxes in Mr. Valens' name," the manager said slowly.

"Well, how much would it be to get him one, right now?" Jolene asked, leaning into him a little breathlessly.

"Oh, for a man with his account balance I could give him one for free, right now."

"Wait, my..." Sean started, but Roxy shushed him.

"Then let's do that," Jolene said and guided the man to his chair, and then, as he sat down, she sat right in his lap!

Sean started to growl and Roxy stepped on his foot.

"*Shut up, Sean!*" Roxy growled softly in his hear.

Sean stilled himself, but he honestly did not like seeing Jolene throwing herself at another man. Part of him understood what she was doing, and part of him was contemplating serious violence as 'his' woman flirted with another man.

"Okay, Mr. Valens," the manager said, pulling out some forms, "please put your name and home address in here and sign these here, and then we can go get you a key."

Sean looked at the forms while picking a pen up off the desk. Using his mom's address, as it was the one on his driver's license, he quickly filled out the forms and signed them, handing them back to the manager as he restrained an impulse to do something to the man, as Jolene was getting quite comfortable in his lap.

The oddest part about it, Sean realized after a moment, was that the man didn't even seem to realize Jolene was there.

"Good, all this is in order," he said and standing up, he steered them out of his office and into the back of the bank. Jolene stood nearby him the entire time, but wasn't touching him anymore.

The manager then led them into a vault, which was full of hundreds of small metal drawers, with two key slots on each one. Going to a drawer, he took out a set of keys and gave one of them to Sean, and then led Sean over to one of the rows.

"Box A-sixty-two put your key in the right side lock."

Sean did as instructed, and the manager took a second key, that was on his key ring and put it in the lock on the left side.

"All boxes take two keys to open, as part of our security," he told Sean as he unlocked his side, and Sean unlocked the other, and sliding the box out, he handed it to Sean.

"You don't need any keys to put the box back in, and there are a couple of small tables just outside the vault, if you want to view the box contents in private," he pointed back towards the entrance.

Jolene put her hand on the man, who stopped a moment.

"But the box away, and ask him to show you again," she whispered. "But use the other key this time."

Sean just nodded and put the box back in the wall, letting it lock back in place and then getting out the key he'd inherited from Sampson he looked at it. There was a small number that he hadn't paid attention to before, 'A-twenty-three'.

It only took a moment to find the box, and he stuck the key in and unlocked the right side.

"Could you open it again for me, please?" Sean asked, "I just want to be sure I'm doing it right."

The bank manager looked at Sean and nodded, "Of course!" He put his key in the left side lock, and unlocked that one as well.

"Thank you," Sean said and pulled out the box.

"You're more than welcome, is there anything else I can do for you today?"

"What's my current cash balance?" Sean asked, wondering again about that earlier remark.

"Two hundred seventy-three thousand, one hundred forty-three dollars and some-odd cents."

Sean's eyes got wide and he looked at Jolene who shook her head.

"Could I take out twenty-five thousand, in cash, please?"

"Of course, may I inquire as to why?"

"Lawyer bill, he only takes cash," Sean told him reflexively.

"Of course, I'll have your money when you're ready to leave."

Sean nodded and watched him go.

"I thought you were broke?" Roxy asked, peering at him.

"It wasn't anything I did!" Jolene told the two of them. "I just made him think he was opening Sean's box, nothing more than that."

"Sampson's money," Sean told them. "Remember, Roxy? The lawyer said he'd put Sampson's money in my bank account?"

"I thought you said Sampson was poor?" Roxy replied.

"Yeah, I did. Maybe we should stop by the lawyer's on the way out of here."

"Good point, now, what's in the box?"

"Oh! Right," Sean said and opening the box he looked in it. There were two envelopes, and pulling those out he quickly stuffed them inside his vest. There was also an old Colt 1911, loaded, with an extra magazine, a small but heavy bag of coins that Sean just stuck in his pants pocket, and a blue velvet jewelry box, which Sean put in his other pants pocket.

"What should I do with the gun?"

"Take it of course," Roxy grinned.

Rolling his eyes, Sean stuck it in one of the lower side pockets of his cargo pants, hoping that it wasn't too obvious. Then closing the safe deposit box up, he put it back in the slot.

"One sec!" Jolene said and stopping him, before he slid it back in. As Sean watched she did a quick spell of some sort, and then using the back of her hand, she slid it in until it locked.

"What was that?"

"Getting rid of fingerprints," she smiled. "Just in case."

Sean shrugged and looked at Roxy who also shrugged.

"Well, let's get my money, and then let's go talk to my lawyer."

"Aren't you going to look at any of that stuff?" Jolene asked.

"Yeah," Roxy said, "after all of this, aren't you curious?"

"Of course I am!" Sean said, a little nervously. "But I'd rather do it in the car, after we're away from here. If anyone else knows about the bank, I'd rather not be here when they arrive."

The girls both nodded, and heading out, the manager had a receipt for Sean to sign, and then handed him two banded stacks of hundred dollar bills, and then counted out another fifty.

"Thanks!" Sean said and they quickly hustled out of the bank and getting into the car, Roxy drove, with Sean in the back again.

"So, what is everything?" Jolene asked.

Sean got out the envelopes first, and started to go through them.

"The first one is Sampson's citizenship papers, naturalization documents, an old green card, birth certificate, what looks like the title to his trailer, the rental agreement, and the titles to his car and his motorcycle.

"The second one," Sean stopped and sighed. "Well now I know where most of the money came from. It's his life insurance policy."

"Oh," Jolene sighed and reached back pat his hand.

"So, what's in the box?" Roxy asked.

Pulling the box out, Sean opened it.

"What is it?" Roxy asked from up front.

"It's a chain," he said and pulling it out he looked at it, "a necklace," Sean corrected. It was a heavy chain necklace, made of some brownish non-reflective metal with a very complicated clasp. Halfway around from the clasp there was a stone set in it. A tiger's eye.

"It's heavy chain necklace with a tiger's eye stone in it."

"What!" Roxy said and pulled over to the side of the street, stopping immediately. "Let me see that!"

Sean shrugged and passed it forward and watched, curious as Roxy looked it over.

"I don't believe it!" Roxy said, "I've heard about these, but I've never seen one!"

"What is it?" Jolene asked.

"Yeah, what is it, Hon?"

"It's a lycan necklace. You have to be someone pretty important to get one of these. Most mages and wizards only give them out to their most loyal servants. They're supposed to be very hard to make."

"That still doesn't tell me what it does, Hon," Sean prodded gently.

"When you shift, it doesn't. It won't catch on anything and can't be seen easily through the fur."

"My clothes don't shift either," Sean pointed out.

"Put it on and shift," Roxy told him, "Trust me, you'll want it."

"I'd rather not have to worry about my clothes right now," Sean chuckled.

"That's the point!" Roxy laughed, "You won't have to. They'll resize to fit you! And when you go full lion? They disappear."

Roxy passed the chain back to Sean and pulled away from the curb.

"Put it on, Sean," Roxy told him. "It's yours now, and you definitely need it."

Sean looked at it. It took a minute to figure out how the clasp worked, and once he did, he put it around his neck.

"Why would Sampson put something like this in a safety deposit box?" Sean wondered out loud.

"Because it's worth a couple hundred thousand dollars to any lycan who doesn't have one," Roxy sighed. "Which is most of them."

Sean blinked, "Then why didn't he sell it?"

"I can give you three guesses, and the first two don't count."

"Huh?"

"Your dad, Sean. Your dad probably gave it to him. Alchemists are the ones who make lycan necklaces. If your dad made that for him, well, selling it would have been like giving up his own child."

"Huh," Sean said and thought about that. "I wonder how hard these are to make?"

"No idea," Roxy said.

Sean looked at Jolene, who was watching him.

"Don't ask me," Jolene shrugged, "I'm not an alchemist or an enchanter. Don't you have a book on enchanting in your head somewhere?"

Sean stopped and thought about that a moment. "Actually, yeah, I think I do. Oh!" Sean stopped and dug out the money in his pocket. Opening up one of the banded stacks of hundreds, he counted off fifty and handed it to Jolene.

"Here, take that."

Jolene looked up at the money and then gave Sean a look that wasn't at all friendly.

"Are you trying to *buy* me? *Sean?*"

Sean snorted, "Didn't you hear the growling when you sat in that guy's lap? I already *own* you, Hon," Sean winked at Jolene as her expression when from pissed to surprised, followed by embarrassed in half a second. "That's just walking around money. Can't let one of my woman go walking around broke, now can I?"

"Hey, where's mine!" Roxy laughed from the front seat.

Sean reached around and set the other half of the stack on Roxy's lap, which Roxy scooped up with a free hand and quickly stuck it in her pocket.

"I think you broke her," Roxy chuckled and tipped her head towards Jolene.

Sean looked at Jolene who was looking at him with a wide-eyed expression of disbelief.

"I think you're right," Sean agreed.

"Oh come on, Jolene, just admit it. You haven't slept with anyone other than Sean since Wednesday, or I'd have smelled them on you. That's gotta be a record for you! Five whole days of monogamy!"

Jolene sighed, turned back around to face forward in the passenger's seat and stuck the money into her pants pocket like Roxy had, instead of her purse.

"You are an *evil* man, Sean."

"Yes, but you love me anyway!" Sean grinned and leaning forward he kissed the back of her head.

"Yes, yes I do," Jolene sighed and smiled.

"Well, we're here," Roxy said, and pulling off the street she parked the car.

"Sean, this is a surprise," Anthony Barton said looking up as Sean, Roxy and Jolene entered the room. "What brings you here?"

"Well, last Thursday someone blew up Sampson's house, my mother's house, and set fire to the place I was living at."

Barton nodded, "I heard about Sampson's and your mother's. A Detective Schumer called me. Says he's been trying to talk to you, but that you seem to have disappeared. I told him I hadn't heard from you."

Sean nodded, "Yeah, there're a lot of people looking for me, and well, none of them are good. But I've been thinking, and as I've become a very suspicious person the last few days I started to wonder just why did Sampson hire you, of all the people he could have hired?"

"I'm afraid that would be confidential between me and Sampson, I'm sorry, Sean."

Sean nodded again and pulling out the last banded bundle of hundred dollar bills he set it on Barton's desk.

"There's ten thousand dollars there. Thank you for transferring Sampson's insurance money. So now, you're on retainer and you're working for me. I cleaned out his safety deposit box, and I've got the one thing that apparently mattered to him," Sean reached under his shirt and showed Barton the chain.

"So, I'd appreciate a little frank talk here."

Barton looked at Sean and sighed, "I tried to get him to sell that once, you know. The money from it would have definitely made his life, and yours, as well as your mother's a lot easier."

"So you knew what Sampson was?" Sean asked.

Barton nodded, "I came here from Angola with Sampson. He saved my life and the lives of my two younger sisters. He went to work for your father; I went to college and then law school. Because I was one of the few 'mundanes' who knew about lycans, magic users, and all the rest, I was able to set up a pretty good practice helping them when they ran afoul of the law."

Barton snorted, "The ones that care about our laws, that is. So when everything suddenly went bad for your family, Sampson enlisted my help and I became his attorney."

"Then you knew about my father's murder?" Sean growled.

"No, until you came in here and mentioned it, I had no idea. I never knew your father, Sean. I only met him once when he paid for me to represent one of his employees. Sampson never told me what happened, he wasn't one to talk much about things he considered private."

"Who warded this room?" Jolene asked suddenly.

"Oh," Sean said, "this is Jolene. She's with me."

"Sampson bit you, didn't he?" Barton said shaking his head.

"You know about lion-weres?"

"They were pretty common back in Angola. At least they were, I don't know anymore." Barton turned to Jolene, "One of my clients took care of it for me, he also warded my house, and gave me a bracelet to wear that keeps others from spying on me. He was rather worried about others eavesdropping on our conversations dealing with his legal issues."

Jolene sighed, "Sawyer, right?"

"You know him?" Barton looked surprised.

"For a goblin who hates humans, he sure seems to do a lot of business with them!" Roxy laughed.

"He understands the realities of doing business, that's all," Barton chuckled. "As a businessman, like it or not, he has to deal with human laws. I'm not a magic user, which is a plus in his book, I know and work with lycans fairly often, another plus, and I'm a licensed lawyer with a local practice who can appear on his behalf.

"So," Barton said looking at Sean, "why did you come here?"

"I want you to deal with the police and any mundane legal matters I may have, Anthony. Sooner or later I'm going to have trouble with the police, because of all the crap that's falling on my head right now. Also I need someone to deal with the mess that was my mom's house and Sampson's house. And last of all, if I end up in jail, I need someone to bail my ass out before the people after me blow it up."

"That's a tall order, and it could get pretty expensive you know."

"I have a quarter million dollars in the bank," Sean pointed out.

"A lot more expensive than that," Barton grimaced and shook his head, "there are people in the legal system, or rather in the court system, who know who and what lycans and supernaturals are. They're willing to look the other way, but it's not very cheap."

"I know how to make more of these necklaces," Sean said with a smile.

"Oh?" Barton paused, and then "Oh! Well, once you start making them, I know a number of wealthy individuals who would be more than happy to buy them."

"Really?"

"I always kept a few on the line in case Sampson ever decided to sell his," Barton shrugged, "I owed him, that's why he came to me whenever he needed legal help." Barton pulled out a piece of paper and set it on the desk, then took the stack of bills and put it in the open desk drawer before closing it.

"Now, that's an official document making it clear that you've retained me and that I have power of attorney. Sign it, and I'll take care of everything."

Sean nodded and picking up a pen on the desk, he did so.

"Don't call Schumer back, and don't call me, my phones are probably tapped."

"Isn't that illegal?"

Barton laughed, "This is Reno, Sean. Illegal rarely stops anyone."

"He's right," Roxy sighed. There's always a judge willing to sign anything in this state, for the 'right' reasons."

Barton nodded, "and then they just argue about it in court later. If you need to tell me something, send me a letter, snail mail. Or by messenger service, if it's urgent."

"Mail? You mean regular mail?"

"Yup, anyone messes with that, and the US government will be all over you. They take a dim view of it still. But honestly? Not that many people even consider it anymore. Plus it can't be traced."

Sean nodded, "Good point. How will you contact me?"

"I'll tell Sawyer if it's urgent, but if I need to contact you, odds are I'll know where you are at that point." Barton paused a moment and then added, "Oh, they found Sampson's motorcycle, it was parked near where that van crashed last week. The police towed it thinking it was an abandoned vehicle. Where do you want it?"

"Store it at Bryson's garage. Tell Steve, the manager there, that it was Sampson's and now it's mine. He'll take care of it. Did they find his car?"

Barton shook his head, "No, they didn't, and that's rather peculiar."

Sean closed his eyes a moment, "Have they found my mother yet?"

"No, which is a good thing, it makes it more likely that she's still alive, Sean."

"Thanks," Sean sighed. "Well, I'll be going."

"Good luck, Sean."

"Yeah, I'll be needing it."

"So now what?" Roxy asked as they got back into the car.

"Back home for now I guess," Sean sighed, and then smiled, "Maybe Jolene can spend some time checking out my new muscles!"

Chaos

Sean was lying on the bed, or more appropriately, lying on top of Jolene. It was late and he'd been making love to the girls since before the sun went down, when he heard it.

"What was that?" Roxy asked, sitting up quickly.

"Shit," Sean swore, "get dressed!" and giving Jolene a kiss he dismounted rather quickly and grabbing his pants he pulled them on, then grabbing his holster he put that on next.

"Gather our stuff up, I'll go check it out," Sean growled and shifted into his hybrid form.

Running over to the fire exit, he stopped and listened, he could hear it, there were people coming up the stairs. Grabbing the door he looked around and saw Roxy, also in hybrid form, with her gun out. "Check the other staircase," Sean whispered.

Roxy nodded and ran off. Drawing his gun, Sean carefully cracked the door open, no one was at the top floor yet, but they were close. Sticking the gun in the doorway, he let the door carefully close onto the slide, then using his body to block any light from the small opening he just waited.

They came around the last corner then, and there were a lot of them, and they were all wearing body armor, helmets, and goggles. They stopped at the bottom of the last flight of stairs, in clear view, and the front man made a hand signal to the rest, then held up his hand, fingers open and started closing them one at a time as the others all got ready.

Sean shot him in the face when he got to 'three' and then emptied all eight shots in the magazine into the first five guys, trying for headshots on each. At least two more dropped before the slide on his pistol locked open.

He could hear Roxy opening up at the opposite end of the building then as well, that wasn't good!

Backing away from the door as the people in the stairwell returned fire; he changed magazines quickly and ran back to the room. Jolene was dressed and was shoving stuff into Roxy's backpack.

"Let's go," Sean said and grabbed his own and slung it on his back as Roxy skidded into the room. Looking around there was still some of their clothes in the room and the bed was rather 'sticky' to put it mildly.

"Can you set this on fire?" Sean asked Jolene.

"Easily!" she smiled.

"Torch it, I don't want them having anything of ours to track me or identify you."

"Sure!" Jolene tossed the backpack to Roxy who caught it easily and slung it on her back.

"Where to?" Roxy asked looking around.

"Elevators, and quickly before they get their act together," Sean growled, and sticking his head out of the doorway, he took a couple shots back towards the door to the stairwell, Roxy doing the same as he felt a sudden wash of heat behind him.

"Come on!" Sean said, grabbing Jolene and taking off for the elevators.

Only two of the four elevators in the building ran all the way up to the top penthouse floor. Sean pried the doors open to one of them rather easily, while Roxy picked off anyone trying to sneak up on them.

The moment Sean got the door open however; gunfire came up the shaft, forcing him back. As both shafts were connected, trying the other one was pointless.

"How far can we fall and survive the impact?" Sean asked as he quickly moved over to the other end of the elevator alcove and started watching out for anyone coming from the other side, from the other stairway. This wasn't good at all. Other than the elevators and the stairways, there weren't any other ways down!

"Not this high! And Jolene would never make it."

"Shit!" Sean swore and just then someone popped their head out as he watched, ducking back quickly as Sean took a shot at them, missing and hitting the plaster just behind where their head had been.

"Damn!" Roxy swore, "They're moving in from this end! Now what?"

"Both stairwells blocked, elevators, blocked," Sean mumbled and tried to remember just how many ways there were up to the penthouses.

"Keep setting fires," He mumbled to Jolene and the next time the guy popped his head out, Sean nailed him, the guy's brains making a nice red and chucky mess on the wall behind him.

"Man, housekeeping is gonna...."

Housekeeping! Sean realized. There was a separate service elevator at the north end of the tower, behind the other stairwell. They'd just have to fight their way to it.

Sticking his hand in the lower cargo pocket, the other pistol was still there. Ripping it out, he took it in his left hand and stuck the magazine in his waistband.

"Listen up!" Sean said in a low voice, "We have to fight our way past the guys at this end. I'll go first. Roxy, cover our rear. Jolene, keep your head down and wait until I clear things out."

"Wait, what?" Roxy asked, "What are you doing?"

"No time!" Sean said and charging out of cover he started to take shots with the pistol in his left hand to keep their heads down, while aiming with the one in his right.

Coming around the corner, there were eight of them, and they were all well armed, and armored.

Sean shot the ones at the back of the group first, as they weren't holding guns, and he had no idea just what magic might do to him. However while he was shooting them, the ones in front opened up on him.

The pain was excruciating. His chest lit up with fire, and suddenly he lost the use of his right eye. Roaring in pain he just dropped the pistols and grabbed the man in front of him and ripped his head off. The next man he disemboweled with a rake of his foot claws, his foot having come up under the man's armor when Sean kicked him as his whole upper body and arms burned with pain like fire.

The two at the back had dropped from his shots, and the four in the middle panicked as they suddenly realized that their buddies were dying.

One of them shot the man in front of him as he peed himself. Sean just grabbed the man before him and bit his face off, then threw him at the two who were now the only ones left standing. One of those two suddenly blossomed into a human torch and screamed loudly as the last one, who had started gibbering just stood there frozen as Sean punched him in the throat, causing him to choke and collapse.

"Sean!" Jolene cried out in shock, "Sean! They shot Sean! It's bad!"

Sean fell to his knees, and gasped for breath. Everything hurt, especially his right eye, which felt like a red-hot poker had been stuck in it.

"Pick up his gun," Roxy growled at Jolene as she came around the corner.

"Was any of it silver?" Roxy growled in his ear.

"How can you tell?" Sean gasped and then coughed up a bunch of blood, and something hard, and solid. Spitting it out he saw bullets hit the floor.

"It feels like your soul is on fire," Roxy grunted, lifting him up. "Set everything on fire here, Jolene. Cremate the bodies and follow me!"

"That way," Sean motioned with his right arm, which had large pieces of flesh now hanging from it. He could even see the bone in spots.

Roxy dragged him to the hallway that the stairs opened out onto, firing a couple of shots that way to keep anyone else's heads down, then moved him past the opening as Jolene sprinted by to keep up.

"Now what?"

"Housekeeping," Sean said as blurry vision started to return to his right eye.

Roxy nodded and kicked in the door.

"The service elevator?" Jolene said coming in the door behind them.

"No one ever thinks about it," Sean nodded and leaned up against the wall leaving a bloody smear as Roxy went over and pried the doors open.

"Well, no one is shooting at us. I'll go down first," Roxy said and jumping into the shaft grabbed the cable and started to slide down it.

Shrugging off his backpack, Sean got his Desert Eagle back from Jolene and stuck it back in the holster after releasing the slide. He'd need to reload magazines later.

"On my back," He grunted and standing up he bent over a bit as Jolene scrambled up on his back and wrapped her arms around his neck.

Picking up his pack he grabbed one of the straps with his teeth and then just jumped into the shaft and grabbing the cable he started to slide down as well. The pain from his hands was tremendous, and with his body still healing from all the bullet wounds, Sean could tell that he was quickly approaching the limits of his healing power.

"Can you do anything about my hands?" He growled, dropping the backpack.

"Not until we get to the bottom. Sorry, Hon."

Sean just nodded and growled.

By the time they got to the bottom of the shaft, Roxy had opened the trap door on the top of the elevator, and grabbing his backpack had jumped down inside. Sean followed, a lot slower, his bloody hands making it difficult for him to grip anything.

"We're in the basement," Roxy said softly as Sean followed her out of the elevator. Jolene slipped off his back and started casting something.

"What's that?" Roxy asked.

"I'm feeding some of his power back into him," Jolene panted and then put her hands on Sean, causing his whole body to light up with a hot, but not uncomfortable, feeling and causing him to sway a moment.

"And now I'm spent," Jolene sighed and sagged a bit.

Sean blinked his eyes, he could see just fine now. Grabbing Jolene he tossed her over his shoulder and looking behind him, he saw a couple of bloody lycan paw prints from his hybrid form. Using his bare feet he quickly smeared them up, and then headed off towards the sub-basement.

"Where are we going?" Roxy asked.

"Sewers," Sean growled.

"You're kidding me!" Roxy said and made a face at him.

"I don't want to go back upstairs, do you?"

"Not really," Roxy sighed, "Sewers it is."

They got to the entrance before any of them heard anyone entering the basement from above, of course the sounds of the fire alarms that were now going off on the floors above and throughout the building could be drowning them out.

"Do you think they know where we're going?" Sean grunted and wrinkled his nose as he opened the access way to the sewers.

"I'm sure they'll figure it out soon enough," Jolene murmured from on his back. "I'd ask you to put me down, but right now I don't want to be stepping in what you two are!"

"Lucky you," Roxy said and shifted back to her human form. "At least like this, it doesn't smell as bad."

Stepping into the sewers behind her, Sean closed the hatch behind him, and then shifted as well.

While the smell was definitely more bearable this way. The feelings of what he was stepping on with his bare feet was not.

"Which way?"

"Upstream," Sean grunted.

"Why?"

"Because this place is gonna get flooded when the water from the sprinklers kicks in."

"Oh!"

They walked the next half-hour or so in silence, that was only broken when Sean coughed up another bullet, followed by the sound of him spitting it out.

When they finally stopped, it was by a metal rung ladder that ran up to a manhole cover.

"Damn, how may of those are you going to cough up?" Jolene asked as Sean paused halfway up the ladder to spit out another one.

"Oh, trust me, he's going to be crapping them out later tonight as well," Roxy grumbled from above them on the ladder. "The body pushes them out to the closest space, and if you don't spit them out, you crap 'em out."

"You've seen it with your dad?" Sean asked.

"No, I've experienced it personally. Which is why *I* don't let myself get *shot* anymore!" Roxy growled.

Sean winced at that tone of voice, and even his lion wanted nothing to do with that statement.

"Um, yeah," Jolene said from her spot between the two of them on the ladder.

"Okay, let's see where we are," Roxy grunted and pushed the manhole cover up and over.

"Better check your ward," Jolene warned.

Sean paused and did just that, recasting his spell. The one from this morning had weakened from the drain on his system, though it was still going. He'd really have to work on that firewall spell he was thinking about, as it wouldn't take any real energy at all.

"Looks like we're in a neighborhood," Roxy said and then pulled herself out of the manhole.

"Hurry up, let's get out of here before a car comes!" Roxy said and reaching down she grabbed Jolene's arm and pulled her up out of the hole, with Sean scrambling out behind her.

Replacing the cover, Sean took his backpack from Roxy and sighed; it was covered in dried blood and pretty badly shot up.

"So, where are we?" Jolene asked looking around as they moved out of the street and onto the sidewalk.

"The sign says Carlin Street," Roxy said, pointing at the street sign as they came up to the intersection.

"If we go south," Sean pointed, "We can get to the river and clean off all this blood and," Sean looked at his bare and very filthy feet, "crap."

"Or we can go to the Gateway Inn back that way," Jolene pointed, smiling, "and get a nice *clean* room with a shower and hot water."

"If I walk in there like this," Sean sighed, "they'll call the police."

"They have balconies. I get a room, you two can jump up."

"Well...."

"They have onsite laundry," Jolene pointed out.

"I don't... Ow!" Sean stopped and looked at Roxy who had just kicked him.

"Let's go. I want to get clean," Roxy growled.

Fifteen minutes later, they had a room on the third floor. Jolene had paid cash up front, and told Roxy and Sean later that the guy at the front desk had seen her here before. He thought she was a working girl, and as she had tipped him well, he'd keep his mouth shut and not call the police or his boss if he discovered extra people in her room.

"You two hit the showers first," Jolene said, wrinkling her nose and pointing at the bathroom the moment Sean and Roxy stepped through the sliding door from the balcony.

Roxy growled a little, surprising Sean, but he kept his mouth shut and just followed her inside. Not saying anything as Roxy got the water adjusted, grabbed the soap, and then stepped into the shower with Sean following.

"Let me scrub your back," Sean said as she stared soaping herself up.

Roxy passed him the soap, but didn't say anything, and as soon as she was done, she stepped out of the shower and started drying herself off.

Sean took a couple of minutes longer, and then getting out and drying himself off he walked out into the bedroom. Roxy was standing there, tapping her foot, with a towel wrapped around her.

Sean sighed, "What?"

She kicked him in the shin, and as he went 'ow!' she hit him across the chin with a right cross that staggered him back against the wall. She'd hit him harder than Dean!

In a low, quiet, and *very* growly voice Roxy took a step forward and got right into his face, "Sean Valens, if you ever, *ever* do something that stupid again, I promise you that you will not only never touch me again, but that I will personally dig you up out of whatever hole they stick your body in and beat the ever loving shit out of you into the next five lives do you understand me!"

Sean blinked, "What the hell did I do?" he gasped, grabbing his jaw. He could feel the bones re-knitting! She'd broken it!

Roxy grabbed the chain around his neck and yanked his face down to hers, his lion had just started to growl and she cut that off too.

"And don't you *dare* growl at me! I'm your damn wife, your woman, *your* mate! If you go off and do harebrained stupid shit, you had damn well better expect to face the music! Do you hear me! And that goes for your lion too! Understand!"

Sean mutely nodded his head, he'd never seen Roxy so angry before, and right now it was all focused directly on him. Even his lion had suddenly realized that shutting up and taking it was the prudent thing to do.

"Do you know how close you came to dying?"

"But we regenerate!" Sean said shocked.

"Not if they cut your head off, you don't! Do you know how close you came to being taken down? There's a limit to how much damage you can soak up at once! What if one of them had silver? Did you even think of that?"

"But, we were running out of time," Sean said softly. Roxy still had a death grip on the chain; he was surprised it hadn't broken. Obviously it was made of pretty strong stuff.

"We still had enough time for you to tell me what we needed to do and for the two of us to take them on, *together*! I could have flanked them, and between the two of us you wouldn't have gotten shot *forty* or *fifty* times!

"Do you *understand* what I'm saying, Hon?"

Taking a deep breath and sighing, Sean nodded, "I'm sorry, Hon. I panicked. I didn't know what to do, I thought we were trapped and I was afraid we were all going to die."

Sean staggered backwards as Roxy, now sobbing, released the necklace and threw herself at him, and wrapped her arms and legs around him.

"You scared me so much! When Jolene said you were shot, the panic in her voice, I was *terrified!* I saw all that blood and thought you were dead! Do you have any idea of just how much you mean to me?"

Looking down at Roxy, Sean honestly didn't know what to say. Putting his arms around her and holding her tightly he slowly dropped to his knees and leaned back against the bed, trying to steady himself. His body was completely drained, he could feel it.

"I'm sorry, Roxy. I love you, utterly, totally, and completely." Glancing up at Jolene, Sean gave her a weak smile, "You too, Jolene. Don't think you're not a part of this or a part of me either."

Jolene nodded slowly. "I, I have to say that I was as terrified as Roxy. I know you guys can heal, but, well, you had a big hole in your head where your eye was, it was..." Jolene gulped, "I think I need to use that shower now!" and she ran into the bathroom.

Sean just stayed where he was, holding onto Roxy, until she stopped sobbing and was just clinging to him.

"Let's go to bed, alright, Hon?" Sean said to her.

Roxy gave a small nod, and carefully getting back to his feet, he carried her over to the bed, and climbing under the covers he just sighed and relaxed, thinking about what had happened.

It could have been the end of him. It probably *should* have been the end of him, and the girls.

Worst of all, he should have known better! He picked a place with no easy escape, no defenses, nothing. He'd been playing RPGs and stuff for ages now, and tactics were tactics. If he'd done those things in a game, made those mistakes, his friends would have teased him for months!

Looking down at Roxy, who had fallen asleep while still clinging to him, he realized he'd just been letting events carry him along, and the only thing he had taken charge of was the girl's bodies. Yeah, sex was great, but if he wanted to keep having it, he needed a safe place to protect not only himself, but what was his.

When Jolene came out of the bathroom, still damp from her shower, she turned out the lights and slid into bed behind him, cuddling up against his back. The clock on the desk said it was almost four; sunrise would be in a few hours. But he didn't have the time to sleep; it was time to start learning. Seriously learning. Reaching over Roxy he grabbed his watch and slipping it on his wrist, he concentrated on the classroom.

Learning the Rules

The first thing Sean did was to start work on his new 'firewall' spell. He'd need to learn a few things to do it. So he made a list of what each of those things was. Attaching a spell to a body took a little work, but not as much as he had thought. There was a book called 'Physical Enhancements' that allowed one to make changes to your own body. That let him figure out just how to put the firewall on himself.

Then in the 'Enchanting Ways' book he found ways of making such changes permanent. Visualizing the program, he took the time to work it all out, just like a firewall program, and even gave it the ability to open 'ports' on command, so that Jolene could cast her mind magic on him again if he ever needed to remember something he'd forgotten.

When Sean had finally gotten it all figured out, he cast the spell on himself, and banished the warding spell that protected him from scrying, and watched as the 'pings' from the scrying spell for a while. There was only one person searching for him this far outside of downtown, and their spell was now blocked, it simply didn't get through to him to cause a response.

Smiling he picked the enchantment book back up and started looking for ways of attaching spells to inanimate objects. That turned out to be easier than attaching a spell to him, but it also took more power, because you had to create a power tap on the object.

Magical objects could draw power from several different places Sean learned. The first was from the person using the item itself. That was fine for non-magical folks, because they couldn't use their magical potential, as small as it might be, anyway. But magic users didn't like that, so other ways had been devised. The most common was for a device to recharge by just sucking energy out of the world surrounding it. It was slow to do it that way however, which explained how some objects could only be used at daily intervals, or even longer if the spell took enough power.

The next was to tap the item into a ley line, where it could pick up power at a vastly increased rate. But that also tied it to the line, so it couldn't move.

There were magical batteries that you could charge, but they didn't carry much energy and were fairly difficult to construct.

And then there were chemical reactions, you could certain magical compounds, and basically decompose them, taking the energy from the decomposition, like say when an organic substance was digested. Those objects were similar to batteries, only you didn't recharge them by putting them on a ley line or casting magic into them. You recharged them by filling them with a special substance to be consumed. Almost like a magical gasoline. However making or finding the proper compounds was neither cheap, nor easy.

The only hitch he ran across was that when enchanting an item, the quality of the physical item itself, had an effect on the quality of the spell. Looking at the chain around his neck, Sean cast an examination spell that he had found in the

Enchanting Ways book, and started to look at just how the spells on it had been laid down.

And there were spells on it, a lot of spells. Spells to protect the chain itself from rust or wear, or even breaking. Spells for it to slowly suck power from its wearer in minute amounts, and store them for later use. There were resizing spells, for both the chain and any clothing worn on the user's body, and a storage spell for anything that wouldn't fit when you changed, however Sean could tell that there were limits to all of these things as well.

Sean could see where it would take days, probably weeks, to lay all of those spells down, effectively coding them each into the item to be enchanted. One after the other. The spells on physical objects had to be put down in a certain order, not unlike a file system being built up in....

Sean blinked. Surely it couldn't be *that* easy! Pulling out a piece of 'paper' in the classroom, he quickly sketched out an archiving program, or rather an archiving spell, that would read everything off of a item, starting from the top and work its way down to the bottom, and create an 'archive' of the object he was looking at.

In effect a tape archive file, a tarball!

Looking it over he examined it several times, and then pointing it at the chain on his neck he let it run, and watched as an 'archive' spell was created. It was massive compared to the other spells he'd learned so far, so pulling up his character sheet he looked at his mental points. Where he'd had two before, he had three now, and he pumped them all into his memory stat, to help with his spell retention abilities, and then went back to look at what he'd created.

Sean assigned it a name, 'Lycan Collar Tarball' and watched as his mind classified it. All he needed was an item to play it back into, and energy of course. Right now, all of the commands in the spells were non-functional because he'd just made a stripped down copy of them, just like an archive program made a compressed copy of a program, which couldn't be run.

How much energy would it take to play back this little tarball of his?

Sean wasn't sure, but he suspected it would be more than he had, and the consequences of not having the energy weren't lost on him. They could be dire.

Feeling someone tugging on him, Sean put it all away and exiting his classroom, he opened his eyes.

Jolene was smiling at him.

"Hey stud, feeling like a little recharging?" she whispered in his ear.

Sean looked over at Roxy, who was still out like a light as Jolene reached down and fondled him.

Rolling over, Sean took Jolene's head in his hands and kissed her deeply, as she spread her legs and guided him into her.

"Somebody is needy," Sean whispered.

"Somebody not only needs a recharge, but they want to be reminded that you're still very much alive," Jolene murmured back, between kisses.

Smiling Sean started to move against her, when suddenly Jolene's eyes got wide.

"What?" Sean asked surprised.

"Your energy! It's gone!" Jolene gasped.

"Wait, what?"

"I'm not getting anything from you, I can't even feel it!"

Sean blinked, "Wait a moment," casting the spell to bring up his 'firewall' controls only took an instant. It was only a few seconds more to add 'grant Jolene all' to the permissions 'file'. As an after thought he added Roxy as well.

"Whoa! What happened?" Jolene gasped.

"I opened a port in my firewall for you," Sean chuckled and went back to kissing her, and moving his body against hers.

"Firewall?" Jolene asked, her legs coming up to wrap around his hips.

"My new warding spell," Sean whispered.

"Oo! Can I take a look?"

Sean smiled down, "Of course you can!"

"Then pick up speed, I need a bit more mana if I'm going to go looking inside your head."

"Such a slave driver," Sean teased.

"Mush!" Jolene giggled, kicking his butt with her heels.

Sean leaned down to nibble Jolene's ear as he complied with her wishes. He still had the spell open, and looking at it, he could see her 'feeding' off him, draining off his own mana. It was rather interesting to watch, because sex improved his vitality and disposition, fulfilling a primal need, so he was actually recovering mana at about half the rate she was draining it.

"It's always like that," Jolene whispered in his ear.

"Ah, you're in my thoughts now," Sean chuckled.

"Of course! I like it here, your lust and love for me is so honest, it's refreshing. So that's your new spell? Ooo, that's pretty neat! Can I copy it?"

Sean stuck his tongue in Jolene's ear and she started to pant.

"You can copy spells from someone's mind?" Sean whispered, a little surprised.

"When they're sharing them like this? Of course! So, can I?"

"Of course you can my hot little tantric sexpot! Maybe you can show me a few spells of your own?"

"You'd have to be in my mind to see them, and mind magic like mine is rare, another reason why they all hate me."

"I don't hate you," Sean purred.

"I don't hate you either," Roxy added and Sean felt Roxy's hands start to run all over Jolene's body as Roxy started in on Jolene's other ear with her tongue as well.

Sean almost laughed as Jolene's body shivered and she tightened down on him quite a bit, hastening the approach of his orgasm. He hadn't closed the spell yet, and suddenly he could see Roxy's energy joining the flow of his into Jolene.

That piqued his interest rather severely, but before he could ask Jolene about it, he was there himself, shivering through his own release.

"My turn," Roxy said as Sean finally wound down.

"Oh definitely," he laughed.

Pulling Roxy close he started to kiss that nice hard body of hers, working his way down its length until he got to her sex, and then started in on her with his tongue. He'd need a few minutes to recover, but that didn't mean he couldn't please her until he did.

Of course Jolene joined in, and when Sean finally mounted Roxy, putting her legs over his shoulders as he made love to her a lot more physically than Jolene tended to prefer, he noticed once again the flow of energy from the two of them into Jolene.

When Sean finally collapsed onto a very satisfied Roxy, who had her legs crossed behind his neck at this point, he pulled Jolene close as they all snuggled, and he shut the spell down.

"Is there anyway you can send all that energy back to me?" Sean asked, catching his breath. "That is what Roxy is giving you, as well as yours?"

Jolene gave a small nod. "Of course. I did that to you last night, remember? But why?"

"Because I can make a copy of my necklace," Sean smiled, "and I want to make one for Roxy. But it takes a lot of energy, about twice what I've got myself I'm guessing."

"What? I thought making one of those took weeks?" Roxy asked.

"Yeah," Jolene agreed.

"I found a shortcut," Sean sighed and nuzzled Roxy. "But it needs all the energy at once. Well, that and a good quality chain."

"So, where's a jewelry store?" Roxy purred happily.

"Boomtown is far enough away that hopefully no one is looking for us, and they got jewelry," Jolene said.

"Two things," Sean said, "first, we need something sturdy like what I'm wearing, they're not going to have that at Boomtown, we'd be better off getting a choker chain at Cabella's, and I don't think I'd survive giving something like that to one of my wives."

"And the second?"

"We don't have a car."

"Oh."

"Yeah, oh."

Roxy tapped Sean on the shoulder and unwrapped her legs from around his neck.

"Let me up."

Sean carefully untangled himself from Roxy and Jolene, and then watched as Roxy got out her phone and started messing with it.

After a minute Roxy smiled, "There's a pawn shop not all that far from here, we can walk there and see what they got."

"What about food?" Sean asked.

"There are tons of food places around there too."

"Sounds good to me then," Sean yawned and stretched, then getting up he looked at his pants from last night.

"I think washing these is a lost cause."

"What about your backpack?"

Sean sighed and nudged it with his foot. "Maybe I should have dropped it before I tried playing kamikaze; it's covered in blood and pretty badly shot up."

Bending over he picked it up, and opening it, he dumped it out on the bed.

"Oh my poor laptop," Sean sighed, it had two bullet holes in it now. Pulling out his clothes, there was one pair of pants in the backpack; the other one was now burned up, along with several of his shirts. There were however two pairs of the canvas shoes and one pair wasn't even shot up. As for his shirts, well, he had a t-shirt and a button down shirt that were both the same color, so if he put them both on, hopefully the holes wouldn't be noticeable.

"Well, let's go shower. Then we can throw the rest of this out and figure out our car problems."

"Are we coming back here to enchant the necklace?" Roxy asked.

"You know," Jolene said. "There's a CVS right next door. Why don't we go there and see about buying Sean some shirts that don't look all shot up first?"

Roxy sat up straight, "There's a convenience store here?"

"Yeah, why?"

"Do they sell like, hair dye and makeup?"

Jolene grinned at her, "Thinking about a makeover?"

"Hell yes! If they can't scry him, or track him, they have to identify him by looks! Well, what if he no longer looks the same?"

Jolene stood up and started getting dressed. "You two shower, I'll go get some makeup and hair dye."

By the time they were done showering, Jolene was back from the store and she tossed Roxy a box.

"I'll be in the shower; you can get started on that."

"Thanks!" Roxy said looking at it, and then at Sean, "Hmmm, yeah, you'll look different as a blond."

"Don't forget the eyebrows!" Jolene warned.

"You're going to dye my hair?" Sean asked.

"Yup. Now grab a towel, this shouldn't take too long."

Sean shrugged and getting a couple of towels he sat down on a chair as Roxy went to work on him.

An hour later, after he'd washed the dye out of his hair, and Jolene had used a pair of clippers on him, he was fairly blond with a lot shorter hair.

"Here, wear these," Jolene handed his a pair of lightly tinted glasses next.

"What are they?"

"Computer glasses, but the look enough like prescription ones that folks will think you need them. Now just a little makeup to make it look like you've got a small blemish on your left cheek, and there! No one will recognize you."

Sean stopped and looked in a mirror, "Are you sure about this?"

"Most people looking for you will either be going by a description, or a picture. Trust me; you're not going to stand out. Now, I need to raid some of Roxy's clothes, and then we can get going."

Sean nodded and put on his pants, socks, and shoes. Jolene threw a large oversized t-shirt at him and he put that on instead of the button down shirt he was thinking of wearing. Jolene had taken a razor to that shirt and when she got done with it she put it on and it was rather hard for Sean to keep his eyes off of her.

"They won't be looking at you, if they're looking at me," she smiled.

"So, everyone ready?" Roxy asked, having cleaned up the mess in the room and stuffed everything they were trashing in Sean's backpack, while Sean had reloaded his two magazines. He'd need more ammo soon. And more magazines, two definitely were not enough.

"What's in the small sack, anyway?" Roxy asked, picking it up off the bed and tossing it to him.

"A dozen gold coins," Sean said, catching it and putting it in his pants pocket.

"That's gotta be about twenty grand right there."

Sean nodded, "Yeah, let's get going."

Two hours later they were sitting in a fast food restaurant eating lunch. They'd found three heavy chains that would work, that were white gold. There were about a dozen more he could have used, but they were made out of silver, and Sean was quickly learning to avoid silver. Touching it didn't damage him, immediately at least, but it was seriously uncomfortable.

"We need a car," Jolene sighed.

"It would definitely help," Roxy agreed.

"We also need a place to stay," Sean added, "a safe place. One with a lot more escape routes."

"I wonder how they found us? That place was warded, right?" Roxy asked, looking at Jolene, who nodded.

"Yeah, it was. I'm guessing that they must have started searching all the buildings in the area, and when they found the tower was warded, they figured that was where you were hiding out."

"You can tell if a place is warded?" Sean asked.

Jolene nodded, "If you're inside it, yeah, of course you can. You just can't tell from *outside.* They must have guessed you were living nearby, after what happened in McDonalds."

"We still don't even know who they were," Sean sighed.

"And we don't know what the ones who got away figured out," Roxy added.

Jolene sighed, "I need to go visit Sawyer."

"*We* need to visit Sawyer," Sean told her.

"Hon, I don't exactly trust Sawyer not to sell us out."

"What, even after my dad paid him that little visit?" Roxy grinned.

"Sawyer's greed often outweighs his good sense, Hon," Jolene pointed out.

Sean smiled, "So, we appeal to his greed. I give him a lycan necklace to sell, and promise him a lot more trinkets after things quiet down."

"Hmm, that might work."

"Now, how about we find a nice place to work a little magic?" Sean winked at the two of them.

"Oh, there's a nice place just down the block from here!" Jolene smiled.

Roxy looked at her, "Girl, do you know the location of *every* hotel in this town?"

Jolene blushed rather suddenly, "Umm, tantric witch, remember?" she said in a very quiet voice.

"With all the things you do to me in bed, it's kind of hard to forget!" Sean purred and then laughed, as Jolene suddenly looked proud, while blushing all the way down to her nicely displayed cleavage at the same time.

"Okay," Sean told them as they got onto the bed, "while I'm fairly sure I understand the theory, I've never enchanted anything before, and I don't know that anyone has done it this way, either.

"So, Jolene, you're the expert here. If things look like they're going too crazy, see if you can't throttle it back, or at least cut you and Roxy out of the feed. I don't want you two getting hurt, okay?"

Jolene nodded, and Sean smiled looking her nicely curved naked body over once again. Leaning forward he pulled her close and gave her a hug and a deep kiss. Then releasing her, he turned and smiled at Roxy, with her more muscular and sleek body and pulling her close he gave her a hug and a long lingering kiss as well.

Jolene had told them which position she felt would give him the most power and control over what was going on, while allowing her to keep an eye on what they were doing. He'd be on his back again, while the girls made love to him and each other. Only this time he'd be holding one of the necklaces they'd bought in his right hand.

Sean almost had to laugh at Roxy's excitement. He wondered which she wanted more right now, him or the necklace? He decided his ego was better off not knowing.

They started off slowly, with the girls kissing and licking at his body, as he let his hands roam over theirs. Sean was already ready to go; just the sight of their nude bodies was enough to excite him. But Jolene had told him that the more pleasure and emotions you brought to the act, the more power you could generate.

Besides, what guy didn't want two unbelievably sexy and powerful women making love to him?

When the girls finally climbed on top of him and they all went to the next level, Sean called up his monitor spell, so he could watch the power flows. Picking up the necklace from where he'd set it on the bed, he got his lycan necklace tarball ready and waited for their power flows to all start peaking.

Just as they did he triggered the tarball to 'download' into the necklace. There was a suddenly surge of power, and the effect was rather interesting as Sean suddenly bucked up hard into Roxy, who was astride him, gasping with a rather powerful orgasm, as Roxy clenched down tightly on him herself, as she also was seized by a powerful orgasm, with Jolene drenching his face as she joined them.

When they all finally came down, Sean took a moment to catch his breath, and give Roxy and Jolene a hug from underneath as they both held each other panting.

"Welcome to the joys of tantric magic," Jolene mumbled.

"Oh, can we do that again?" Roxy purred, having shifted into her hybrid form. Sean was a little surprised that he'd shifted as well. Using his powers he checked the necklace, everything was exactly as it should be, magically.

"I don't see why not," Jolene laughed weakly. "I mean we have two more to do right?"

Sean heard Roxy pick up one of the other necklaces off the nightstand by the bed, and then she took the one he'd just done and handed him one of the regular chains.

"Back to work, Love!" Roxy purred and reaching down gave him a couple of pats on the chest.

Sean growled, but while the power he could see through his magic had decreased some, there actually was more than enough left to do two more. The joining of the three of them had apparently generated a lot more than Sean had realized, and suddenly he understood the real reason the other magic users didn't like tantric practitioners. Jolene and he had just unleashed a very large amount of power, undoubtedly a lot more than regular magic users could muster with only three people.

Grabbing Roxy's thighs, Sean got back to 'work' rather enthusiastically.

An hour and two rather orgasmic experiences later, a fairly exhausted Sean was being washed in the shower by Roxy and Jolene who were being incredibly affectionate.

"That was wonderful," Roxy purred.

"You're just happy that you got a necklace," Sean sighed, relaxing between the two of them.

"Well, yeah!" Roxy laughed, "But that whole experience was nice. It reminded me of the first time all three of us where together."

"It can be a tad habit forming," Jolene agreed. "Though we need to be careful we don't wear our Sean here down to a frazzle. He was supplying a lot of the magical energy."

"You mean our mate," Roxy smiled and hugged him.

Jolene blushed, "Okay, our mate."

Sean purred rather loudly when Jolene said that, and turning to her, he took her head between his hands and kissed her.

"Finally!" Sean smiled.

"Yeah, yeah. My old master warned me that this might happen one day."

Roxy smiled and hugged them both, "Now, what do you say we dry off and get some food into our mate here, then grab a bus or something over to Sawyer's place?"

"It's almost three, will he still be there?" Sean asked.

"He's a fence for the supernatural," Jolene chuckled, "he's *always* there."

"Umm hmm," Sean nodded and took a moment to examine the necklace Roxy was now wearing. Interestingly enough, it was now an exact copy of his, right down to the coloration and the tiger's eye stone in the center. Apparently his tarball archive had copied not just the magical aspects of the lycan necklace, but the physical aspects of it as well.

That gave Sean a few thoughts, but he'd have to consider the implications of that later. Right now he wanted a quick bite to eat, and to go meet this Sawyer.

Small Change

"Guns aren't allowed inside the store," Marx said to Sean as he walked inside.

Sean stopped and looked at the large, well, heavy, almost obese, guy sitting by the door; his lion felt it immediately, wereboar. Big one too.

Sean smiled at him and looked Marx in the eyes and smiled, "Do you really think I need a gun?"

Marx's eyes suddenly went very wide, and he noticed Jolene and Roxy entering behind Sean.

"It's *him*, isn't it?" Marx hissed at Jolene in a whisper.

Jolene just smiled and nodded.

"What are you doing bring him here? Are you crazy?"

"Here, have a gift," Sean said and handed Marx one of the two lycan necklaces.

Marx looked at the necklace and back at Sean, "I can't afford one of these!"

"I said it was a gift, put it on, try it out. I want your boss to be sure I'm selling the real thing here."

Turning back towards the counter at the other end of the room, Sean, started to walk towards it, looking over the small green man standing behind it. Jolene had warned him about Sawyer. Extensively. She told him he was tall for a goblin, even handsome by their standards. But he was still a rude, crass, greedy, and self-serving man, unless he could make a profit, or his personal safety was on the line.

"Hey, Tramp! Why are you bringing filthy humans in here?" Sawyer yelled from the back. "Can't you do your tricks in the alley, like all the other whores do?"

Growling Sean walked up to the counter, eyes level with Sawyer.

"You will *not* refer to my woman like that, understand?"

Sawyer laughed, "Why? You gonna do something about it?"

Sean shifted and looked down at Sawyer, and growled again, "If I have to."

Sawyer's eyes got wide and he looked at Jolene and then at Roxy.

"Shit! You brought Tooth and Claw Channing's kid in here, *and* the Valens' kid? What are you trying to do to me, Jolene! Get out of here! Now! Leave!"

"Well at least you aren't calling her rude names anymore," Sean chuckled and pulling out the other lycan necklace, he put it on the counter. "Know what this is?"

"A cheap necklace, that's what it is," Sawyer said looking at Sean nervously. "You want a pawn shop, there's a thousand of them in this town. Go find one."

"Boss!" Marx said walking up and standing next to Sean, "It's a lycan necklace."

"Sure it is!" Sawyer said.

Marx shifted, and Sean notice that as a hybrid, Marx came up to his nose - he was pretty damn big. Sure, Sean was bigger, but he'd definitely rather *not* tangle with the wereboar.

"Notice my clothing didn't rip?" Marx said.

Sawyer looked at Marx, then back at Sean.

"I gave him one, as a gift," Sean smiled, "so you could prove to any potential customers that you did indeed have a *source*."

Sawyer eyed him warily, "What do you want?"

"Information, lots of it. I need to know who's after me, where they live, what they're doing, what *they're* afraid of, contacts to people who might help me, and a bunch more necklaces like this one to enchant."

"And what do I get?"

"You get that one for free, and we split the take fifty/fifty on the rest of the ones I give you."

"You start spreading these around, and you know the bottom is going to fall out of the market!"

Sean grinned, "That's the idea. And after I flood the market with these, I'll start flooding it with whatever other magic items that the councils don't want lycans to have."

Sawyer paused a moment, and put his hand on his chin in thought, "Let me make sure I have this straight. You want to flood the market with stuff specially designed to piss off the magic users, while I make money in the process?"

Sean nodded, "Something like that."

"I thought lions were supposed to be all about law and order?"

"Yeah, for lycans. We're also pretty damn big on revenge against people who murder our families," Sean growled the last bit out showing a lot of fang.

"Whoa, whoa, kid! I wasn't involved in any of that; I was living in her neck of the woods up until just a few years ago."

Sean nodded slowly, "That's why I'm here talking to you, instead of say, tearing you into little pieces."

"So, you're really gonna pick up your old man's work and stick it to the councils and help the lycans out?"

"Of course. They ruined my life, now it's only fair I ruin theirs as well. They should have just left me alone; I was willing to move on with my life. But they weren't, so what choice do I have?"

Sawyer thought about that, and then nodded.

"You got a deal, Kid," he turned to Marx then. "Anyone shows up, I'm on an hour break." Picking up the necklace Sawyer turned back to Sean, "Come on in the back, better not to have any of you out here, in case someone shows up while we're talking."

Nodding, Sean shifted back to his human form and followed Sawyer through a series of doorways and short halls until they entered a rather nice conference room.

"Have a seat," Sawyer said and took the one at the head of the table, which was raised up to put him on an even footing. "Now, what do you want to know?"

Jolene spoke up then, "First off, who led the attack on us in the tower yesterday?"

"That was Harkins' people. He's pretty pissed over what Sean there did to his guys over the weekend. It made him look weak to his people, so he had to commit to some force."

"How's he feeling after what Sean did to the ones in the tower?"

"Harkins is telling people that while everyone up there got away, that Sean's dead."

"Really?" Sean asked, surprised. Jolene and Roxy looked just as surprised as he was.

"One of their people heard some gal yelling about Sean being shot, really bad, and they couldn't find any traces of him, just a lot of blood. Course they couldn't stick around long with the fire and the fire department on the way, but since then, no one has been able to scry him anywhere, even for an instant. Total blank."

Sawyer looked Sean over a moment, "You must be one hell of a magic user, Kid. You can create powerful magic items, and block the most powerful scrying mages in the city enough that they can't even get an echo out of you."

"So, who is this Harkins?" Sean asked.

"Harkins is the head of the Council of Ascendance. They're one of the weaker major councils, except for out here in Reno; here they're the number two. They believe in the divine right of magic and magic users. They ain't too popular with most of the other councils out there."

"How many councils are there?"

"Five major ones, I think nine minor ones. The major ones are Vestibulum, they're the most powerful and the biggest, Morgan runs their coven here. Next is Sapientia, they're the oldest, they made most of the rules and traditions that everyone follows these days, Troy is the leader of the local coven. Eruditio is all about learning and knowledge, they tend to stay out of politics, so I have no idea who runs their local coven. That leaves Gradatim, they're weaker than the Ascendance crowd, and those two hate each other's guts. McConnell runs them."

"And which of these are trying to kill me?"

Sawyer pondered that a moment, "Well, Eruditio, I doubt they care. Sapientia? If they think you're violating some of their more sacred rules, they might. Vestibulum, they'll want to rein you in, get control of you. If they can't do that, they may decide to kill you, but only if they see you as a threat to the current status quo."

"That doesn't sound too bad."

Sawyer laughed, "Kid, if the rumors about you getting the collective boot of the councils off the lycan necks are true, they'll want you dead, trust me. Same for Sapientia too most likely as making the lycans free probably violates some stupid rule of theirs."

Sean sighed, "I know that the Gradatim want me dead."

"They want your power, they just figure they'll have to kill you to get it," Sawyer pointed out.

"So I take it the guys who did the lightning attack, Totis Viribus, they're a minor council?"

Sawyer nodded, "Yeah, they're pretty much in Harkins' pocket; they're allied with the Ascendants in most places. They're small enough around here that they were able to get two other minor groups to ally with them to cast the spell. Harkins had promised some pretty sweet rewards to those that helped."

"I heard two of the mages involved died?"

"Yup, Preston, the guy leading the Totis, he had a few qualms with the folks from the Sorceress's guild. Seems they found his problems with his ex-wife to be rather humorous and laughed at some point during the casting and resisted his attempts to kill her. So he turned on them as the circle's leader and killed them.

"So now the Sorceress's guild is at war with the Totis, and no one other than the Ascendants will side with them any more for breaking their word."

"So, who wanted my father dead?"

Sawyer shrugged, "Best I know, Kid, they all did. They hired someone from the outfit back in Chicago to come out here and do the job. Honestly, I'm surprised that the locals are going after you themselves."

"They probably thought I was going to be a pushover," Sean sighed, "but the ones who started all of this seems to have been the guys from Lithuania."

"No, they're just the ones who got to you first. I gotta ask you, Kid, what *did* your father leave you?"

Sean thought about that a moment, he didn't want to say 'nothing,' because that would so obviously be a lie.

"He left me a bunch of books on magic," Sean told him, "but I couldn't use them, because someone had put a geas on me. After a couple of the attacks, I got the geas removed."

Sean shook his head, "Like I said, I just wanted to move on. I actually know a *lot* about magic, probably more than most of the covens out here. But I wasn't able to practice it. Now I can."

"So, he didn't leave you something to free the lycans?"

"I don't even know just what the power magic users have over them," Sean admitted. "So if my father left me something, I've totally missed it."

"Hasn't she told you?" Sawyer said and motioned towards Roxy.

Roxy shrugged, "I'm not so sure I understand it myself, I just know it has something to do with silver. My father was never keen on the details and well, our family hasn't been under the sway of any of the councils for generations."

"They implant a ceramic pellet that contains powdered silver, with a spell on it. So all it takes is the proper word, your name, and the ceramic splits, and the silver is dumped into the bloodstream and the lycan involved dies a slow and very painful death."

Sean blinked, "What? Why not go to a doctor and get the pellet removed?"

"It's often placed somewhere hard to get at. Also, a lot of magic users, when dealing with lycans, know to use silver bullets, darts, or cast a cloud of silver particles. Silver has been fairly well weaponized against lycans by the magic community, to keep them under control. They've also spent a lot of time indoctrinating the hell out of as many of them as they can.

"True, not all lycans are controlled nowadays, but enough are that most free lycans know better than to get involved with magic users. If you want to do something to stop that control, you have to do something to remove their weakness to silver."

"And everyone thinks my father had figured out a way to do that?" Sean said, looking Sawyer in the eyes. "That would take a complete understanding of why silver effects them at a biological level, and then the ability to make a retrovirus that altered them enough to block that effect, while still leaving lycans as lycans. You'd need genetic skills that don't even exist in the world today! That's just crazy."

Sean shook his head again. "These people are insane."

"Well, apparently your father did something that convinced all of them that it was possible and that he was going to do it."

Sean sighed, "Maybe if I knew what that was, I'd have an idea of where to start. But right now we need to find a new place to hole up for a while."

"Well you can't stay here!" Sawyer said, "I get too many people coming through here to ever keep it a secret. Hell, I'm hoping Marx doesn't go telling all his lycan friends you came here."

"Why would he do that?"

"Because, you're like the lycan messiah right now, Kid. You're not only the one who's supposed to free them from oppression, but you're one of them too!"

"Damn, any chance on keeping that last bit a secret? Last thing I need is them to start using silver bullets."

"Sorry, Kid. Sooner or later they're going to figure it out, and the odds are on sooner. Once word gets around that Harkins didn't kill you, expect things to go into overdrive. If I were you, I'd lay low for a while."

"Yeah," Sean sighed. "Now about those chains?"

"I have a few more questions first," Jolene interrupted, "starting off with the addresses for the council leaders."

"It'll take me a minute, but I got 'em all on file," Sawyer grinned.

Sean listened only with half an ear as Jolene started asking a lot more specific questions about the smaller councils and a number of people in particular. She also wanted to know if either she or Roxy had been outed yet as the people who were with him.

The score on that seemed to be yes on Roxy, and no on Jolene. So Sean made sure to keep Roxy's protection from scrying spell active. As she couldn't cast magic, she couldn't do the firewall spell. Though maybe if he put it on an object and let her wear it? Sean would have to think about that.

When it finally came time to leave, Sawyer gave them a bag of a dozen gold or gold-plated chains that all looked suitable, and then he showed them out through a back passageway that came out quite a distance away from his shop.

"So, now what?" Roxy asked as they walked out of the industrial park. "It's after five, and the sun's starting to go down.

"We go get a car," Sean said.

"And just how do we do that?"

"Steve's shop is about a twenty minute walk from here, and he's open 'til six."

"And he'll sell you a car?"

"I wouldn't be surprised if he just gave me one," Sean shrugged, "but if not, I've still got almost five grand in cash, a debit card with a lot more money on it, and twelve troy ounces of gold in my pocket. I'm not worried about it."

"Aren't you worried they'll find your friend?"

Sean snorted, "They couldn't find my room off campus for how long? And I was living there for years? They've probably only figured you out because they saw you at the tower, and they still haven't discovered Jo.

"If they were going to bother my mundane friends, I'd think they already would have. But if they're not seen with me, how are they going to know about them? I don't think these people really traffic much with mundanes, or have spells to find out who your friends are, am I right, Jo?"

Jolene nodded, "There aren't any spells to find out who your friends are, or who you know. Unless they're already inside your head. Though I will warn you that they do traffic with the mundanes more than just a little. They have to go to the shops just like we do, after all, and some of them actually do have mundane acquaintances."

Sean nodded, "Point taken."

"So let's not try to stand out too much, okay?"

"Agreed. There's the shop, let's go in the back door," Sean said.

Cutting around to the back, Sean led them in the back way, and went up and cut into the offices for the shop from the back.

"Excuse me, but you aren't allowed back here," a woman behind a desk said.

"Martha, after all these years, you don't recognize me?" Sean teased, taking off the glasses.

"Sean, I swear, what happened to you? What in the world ever possessed you to dye your hair?"

"Long story, is Steve in his office?"

"He's about ready to close up, better make it quick!"

Sean nodded and crossed the room, stepping into Steve's office.

"Steve," Sean said, looking at his friend who had his attention focused on a computer screen.

"Sean! Grab a seat, I'm just finishing up the day's numbers," Steve glanced up and then back at his screen. "And what the hell did you do to your hair and who are those lovely women and why would they be seen with the likes of you?"

"It's a long story," Sean sighed sitting down. "I need a car, preferably one that won't be traced to me right away. I got cash, so I can pay you for it."

Steve made a raspberry sound at him, "Your money is no good here, you know that. You can have one of the shop's loaner cars. Don't worry about it."

Steve did something on his computer and then stood up.

"I gotta close up the shop and send everyone home for the day. Make yourselves comfortable, there's beer in the fridge," Steve pointed at a small cube fridge in the corner.

"Don't tell anyone I'm here, okay?"

"I saw what happened to the house and I've already talked to your lawyer, don't worry, I know you've got problems. Now, take a load off, I'll be back in ten."

Sean nodded as Jolene joined him on the couch; Roxy got a beer first and then sat with them both.

"So how much are you going to tell him?" Roxy asked.

"As much as he wants to know," Sean sighed. "I'm not in the habit of keeping secrets from my friends."

Roxy was on her second beer, and Sean and Jolene had both relented and were on their first when Steve finally came back up.

"Okay, shop's locked up, the customers are all gone, and my mechanics are cleaning up and checking out as we speak. So, tell me, who are these two lovely women and why are they both hanging off of you?" Steve asked with a laugh.

"Everything that's going on and you want to know about my sex life?" Sean sighed shaking his head.

"Well come on, Sean, what's harder to believe? That people are trying to kill you, or that you've actually *got* a sex life now?" Steve grinned, "So, introduce me already."

Sean smiled, "This is Roxy, the hot track star you've heard me talk about, and this is Jolene, the hot friend of Roxy's that I don't know if I've ever mentioned before. Roxy, Jo, this is Steve, my friend from public school, and former partner in crime."

Steve smiled and shook hands with each of the girls, and then dragged a chair over.

"So, inquiring minds wanna know, are all three of you?"

Roxy and Jolene both smiled, "He's our man," Roxy said, "And we're his women," Jolene finished.

"Whoa, seriously?" Steve asked looking at Sean, who blushed and nodded. "Yeah, *very* seriously. A lot has happened in the last week, and they're the only two good things in it."

"Yeah, I can tell that much at least," Steve nodded. "So, on the serious side of things, who's after you, and why? In the last week there's been something of a deadly crime wave in town, as well as quite a bit of arson."

"Yeah, I know," Sean grimaced, "and it all revolves around me."

"Let's start with the why."

"My father didn't die in an accident. He was murdered. He was working on something that a lot of people didn't want to see succeed. So they murdered him, and then set things up so mom and I would be destitute."

"And someone thinks you've discovered his secret, right?"

"That was quick," Roxy commented.

Steve shrugged, "Only thing that would make sense. Sampson's dead, his mom's missing, and there've been multiple attempts on his life apparently."

"That's about the size of it," Sean nodded. "They think my dad left me something and I'm gonna finish his work. They think that he arranged for me to get his notes or something on my birthday."

"Okay, the next question then, who?"

"You're not going to believe me."

"Well, you won't know until you tell me, now will you?"

Sean shrugged. "Okay, try this on for size. My father was a powerful alchemist who was working on a magical device that would free all of the lycanthropes who are in thrall to the magic users, who run a bunch of magical councils and stuff. They didn't want to lose their servants, errand boys, and cannon fodder, so they had him killed. Now they're after me."

"Lycanthropes? Like werewolves?" Steve said sitting back in his seat, "And magic users, like wizards and mages?" Steve tilted his head to the side and gave Sean a rather frank look. "Sean, are you feeling alright?"

"I said you wouldn't believe it, now here's the tough question: Do you want me to prove it, or would you rather believe I'm crazy."

"How do you prove a thing like *that?*" Steve said, looking at Sean like he was crazy.

Sean stood up and pulled his shirt off over his head.

"And just when in the hell did you become so muscular?"

"Part of what happened to me. You see, Sampson was a werelion; he worked for my dad and promised to watch over me and mom when dad was killed. When they tried to kidnap me last week, he rescued me, but I was pretty badly hurt and he'd been shot up with silver and was dying. So in order to save me, he bit me."

"Oh dear lord, you're kidding me!" Steve said. "If you can't prove that right now, I'm calling an ambulance and getting you committed."

Sean shrugged and shifted into his hybrid form.

Steve just sat there a minute, staring at him.

"Well?" Sean asked after a second minute had gone by.

"I'm trying to figure out just what the hell to say next. There's a lot going on here, Sean."

Sean laughed, "How the hell do you think I feel? I'm right in the middle of it! Hell, I'm a lion-were now, Steve. I can turn into a full lion if I want!"

"Seriously?"

Sean nodded.

"Let's see it."

Sean shifted into his full lion form and then blinked as Steve got up and walked over to him and tapped him on the head, then ran his fingers through his fur.

"You know," Steve said looking at him, "I know the booking agent for the Atlantis. I bet we could put together one hell of an act."

"Really, Steve?" Sean grumbled.

"You'd have to be silent though, I don't think the audience would buy a talking lion," Steve looked at the girls, "And are you both?"

"I'm a cheetah-were," Roxy smiled, "Jo's a magic user."

"Can I see?" Steve asked, "Please?"

"You know if you hit on her I'm going to take a bite out of your ass," Sean growled.

"Pfft, Terri would have my balls. No way I'm throwing over my fiancée."

Roxy shifted into her hybrid form and Steve just shook his head, "Wow, you're even better looking with fur. All these years watching anime, and now I finally get to see a real cat girl." Steve shook his head again, "Almost tempted to ask you to bite Terri after the wedding!"

"You're taking this rather well," Jolene observed.

"Eh, coping mechanism. My father always believed in throwing me into the deep end with business and everything else. Said that learning to cope with unexpected events calmly would make me a successful businessman. Don't think I'm not freaking out over here, but," Steven gave Sean's shoulder a push, "it's Sean. I can't go freaking out just 'cause my buddy got into some weird shit. What kind of a friend would I be?"

Sean shifted back to his human self then, and Roxy did the same.

"So, what are your plans?" Steve asked, looking at the three of them.

"To find a safe place to lay low for a while and start figuring out our options while I try to find out if my dad did leave me anything."

"And that's it?"

Sean spread his hands and looked at Steve, "What else is there?"

Steve shook his head, "All those years of playing RPGs and you don't see it? Sean, you're leading a revolt here, and everyone knows it, except for you! You need to plan accordingly!"

"What?!"

"Look you just told me that all of the lycans are living under oppression, you're searching for the key to end that, and you're facing the combined might of a bunch of magic users?

"Tell me that doesn't sound like a revolution? Or at least a kick-ass D&D campaign!"

"Umm,"

Roxy sighed, "He's right, Hon."

"It's definitely how all the councils see it," Jolene agreed.

"See?" Steve said, "They agree. And no one is going to leave you alone, ever, until you win it. Because they're always going to believe you're still fighting them. So, unless you're planning on selling out, which we all know from years of gaming never works, it's do or die.

"Excuse me a minute," Steve said and pulling out his cell phone started texting.

"What are you doing?" Sean asked.

"Telling Terri that I have an advertising issue I need to resolve and I'll be home late. There," Steve set his phone down, "now, tell me everything, and I do mean *everything.*"

Sean shrugged and looked at Roxy.

"Not like we have anything to lose," she said.

"Roxy's right," Jolene agreed.

"Alright, it started the Friday before last...."

It took Sean over an hour to tell Steve everything, or almost everything. He left out the watch, and he didn't go into details on *any* of the sex of course.

"Okay," Steve said slowly, thinking about it for a few moments. Then he turned to Jolene, "Jo, how many magic users, of all types live in the area?"

Jolene shrugged, "Between all of the different councils here, there are probably fifteen hundred or so. Add in another five hundred to a thousand to include family members who are too young, or people who don't affiliate with any of the organized groups, say twenty-five hundred, three thousand, tops."

"So out of the half million living in Washoe and Storey counties, we're looking at less than one-hundredth of one percent of the population?"

Jolene nodded, "Yeah, about that. The ability to work magic is pretty rare, and most folks who can prefer to live in cities, there tends to be more power there. That and they don't like roughing it."

"Roxy," Steve asked looking at her, "how many lycans would you say there are?"

Roxy pondered that a moment, "That's a tougher question, both cause I've only lived here a few years, and we don't organize anywhere near as well as the magic users do, but there are definitely a lot more of us. Probably three or four times as many of us as there are of them, but we're also a lot more spread out. Some lycans like cities, some don't."

"So, less than ten thousand?"

"Umm, probably around that many, but it's just a guess."

Steve nodded, "So less than a tenth of one percent of the population is going to be involved here."

Roxy, Jolene, and Sean all nodded slowly.

"But," Roxy spoke up, "you have to remember that magic users effect a larger amount of control here than the average person. Most of them are rich; quite a few of them have some level of influence with the local politicians because of that."

"And they can cast magic," Jolene added. "That's something of a multiplier. It lets them do things that the mundane can't."

"How many of those magic users are going to be actively looking for you? Actively involved? Ten percent? Twenty? Oh, I'm sure the rest will back them, but you're probably only going to be worrying about two or three hundred people, tops!"

"That's still a hundred times the three of us," Sean pointed out.

"Ah, but how may of the ten or so thousand lycans are willing to be on your side? Ten percent of that is still a thousand people, and I'd suspect that the overwhelming majority will support you when push comes to shove.

"And that leads to the first thing you need to be doing," Steve smiled.

"And that is?" Sean asked, a little skeptically.

"Advertise! There are two things every movement, organization, or business needs! Money and followers. You don't get those by sitting on your butt! Trust me, that's why my mom and dad are sailing around the world while I'm sitting here running the business. You need to advertise."

"We do that, and every magic user in the world is going to be on our case!" Jolene replied.

"It's all in the presentation," Steve grinned. "Sean redoes his facebook page, talks about this epic 'game' he's involved in, and how he's fighting against the forces of evil mages to save the enslaved lycan race.

"Once a week or so, he updates it. Then, you start a go-fund-me campaign, tell everyone you're going to be making like a novel, or a graphic novel to memorize the campaign, that you'll sell or giveaway a ring or a necklace to those who contribute over a certain amount. Say ten grand maybe?"

"But, what if we don't deliver?"

"That's the beauty of go-fund-me versus a kickstarter; you don't have to pay off. But think about it, it lets everyone in the lycan community know you're out there, fighting the fight as you give them weekly status reports, and all they have to do to take part is contribute some cash."

"Yeah, but what happens if mundanes start donating?" Roxy asked.

"That's the whole point!" Steve laughed, "You can fundraise from them too, and no one can ever claim you spilled the beans. You're just some RPG nerd trying to bring his favorite campaign to life! While raising money and recruiting people to your cause right under the enemy's nose."

Sean leaned back against the couch and blinked. Steve had a pretty good point.

"We'll need a website too of course," Sean said slowly, thinking about it.

"Of course."

Jolene laughed, "You know, it'll be weeks if not months before any of the councils tweak to it. They're notorious for not using the internet."

"Stickers," Roxy said, "we need to sell stickers. We can make a bunch of different ones for each of the different lycan races with some logo or phrase on them. We sell them so people can show their support by plastering them all over the place. That'll bring in lots of mundanes, and once the mages see that," Roxy growled, grinning, "they'll fucking freak."

"Just be careful of one thing," Steve warned.

"What?" Roxy growled.

"The goal isn't to get rid of the mages; the goal is to free the lycans. You don't want to drive any mages who are sympathetic to your cause into the arms of the other side."

"He's got a very good point, Rox dear," Jolene said smiling at Roxy.

"Okay, okay," Roxy sighed, giving an embarrassed grin, "We can add a couple of stickers for those magic users who support the cause."

Sean nodded, "Okay, so we have an idea to make money, get the word out there, and rally support, right?"

Everyone nodded.

"So, once we have all that money and support, what do we do with it?"

"You go and talk to Chad," Steve said.

"Chad?" Sean blinked, "Why Chad?"

"Because he's the best damn DM in Reno, that's why," Steve grinned.

"Steve, we're talking real life here, not some game!"

"Oh? Who do you know who has studied war, combat, revolutions, and hell even small uprisings and riots in history, more than Chad?"

Sean had to stop and think about that. Chad was always pulling stuff out of history to throw at them in games to see if they went the same route as history took, or came up with something different. Chad gamed *everything* that he did in life, he'd even opened up a small gaming store that was doing rather well.

"You know, this just keeps getting more and more complicated," Sean sighed.

"It always does."

"So how do we keep in touch?"

"Talk to John about that, he got me an email address on one of those secure email sites a while back. Maybe we should all get a couple of those disposable phones from seven-eleven too."

Sean laughed, "He got me one of those accounts too. Hell, I think he got all of us in the gaming group one. Guess it's time to start using it."

Steve stood up then, "Well, I need to get home, or Terri is gonna kill me," reaching into his pocket he pulled out a set of keys, "These are for the Mercedes wagon in the back. The windows are tinted enough to make it hard to see in, but not enough to get the cops on your butt, and around here it blends in pretty well."

"Thanks, Steve," Sean said standing up and taking the keys, he shook hands.

"Are you kidding? This is gonna be more fun than any D&D campaign we ever played as kids! I miss not being able to play anymore."

Roxy came over and gave him a hug and a kiss on the cheek, making Steve smile, then Jolene did it and actually made him blush.

"Whoa, girl, you trying to get Sean and Terri to kill me?"

Sean sighed, "Jo's a tantric witch, she can't help herself."

"I don't think I needed to hear that," Steve laughed. "Now go, use the back door and I'll finish locking up. Night!"

"Night!" They all replied.

Outta Town

It was late, and Sean was lying back in the bed, panting, with the girls cuddled up to either side of him.

"There has to be an easier way to do this," Sean said slowly as he caught his breath.

"I don't know, this way definitely has a lot to be said for it!" Roxy, laughed. She wasn't panting as hard as Sean was, but her naked body was just as covered in sweat as his. This of course looked incredibly sexy on her, especially as he'd had something to do with getting her that way.

"You're both right," Jolene sighed, "and while I'm all for doing it this way, we'll never be able to keep up with demand. The time alone for each one is just too much."

"What about ley lines?" Sean asked, "Don't they have the power?"

Jolene scowled, "They have power, and you can tap into it, but all of the powerful ones tend to have someone or something living on top of the key points. But I've been watching you work, Sean. Making these things requires a decent amount of energy, but only a third of it gets used. Two thirds of it comes back to us, any way you can at least cut down that upfront amount?"

"No," Sean sighed and gave his head a small shake, "the program needs all of that to function. It has to do with the way the archive is restored. You need the full amount of magical energy when you 'playback' each of the spell components and device functions in order to put them into the item properly. I'm not sure yet why I get as much energy back as I do when the spell completes, I'm still trying to understand all of that. But that initial amount we need is just one drawback of the process."

"Doesn't feel like a drawback to me!" Roxy giggled.

"There has to be another way to tap power," Sean said, thinking about it. "I've seen magical batteries. They don't hold much, but maybe a lot of them built together?"

"And just how much time and energy would that take?" Jolene asked.

"Too much, I'm sure," Sean sighed.

"Maybe you should look through your books and see if your dad left you anything on it?" Roxy suggested.

"That's an idea, but let's get some food first, then maybe a nap."

"After a shower," Jolene said.

"Yeah, definitely a shower," Roxy agreed.

"You two go first, while I build up my strength," Sean teased.

Sean smiled and watched them as they sauntered off to the bathroom, then he called up his monitor spell and checked. They were about an hour's drive east of Reno in a small town, and no one was scrying for him here at all. They'd spent the day enchanting necklaces and now had a dozen of them. Two he'd mail to his lawyer, the other ten he'd mail to Sawyer with instructions to send his cut to his lawyer.

Getting out of bed Sean stretched and shifting back to human he looked at himself in the mirror. He really did look different now, and it wasn't just the blond hair. He was a lot more muscular, to the point where it was obvious to him that he'd changed, and there wasn't a bit of fat left anywhere on him.

Going into the bathroom he leaned against the sink and enjoyed the sight of his wives washing. Sean snorted to himself at that, he didn't know if that came from him or his lion, and he honestly didn't care. They were his now, they knew it, he knew it. He'd have to get them rings so everyone else would know it too.

"So, I've been thinking," Sean said and stretched again.

"Uh-oh, should we be worried?" Roxy teased.

"I need a new laptop, one I can build the website on, then we need to find someplace with a good internet connection, so I can find a good hosting service to set it up, then update my facebook page, and then setup that go-fund-me campaign."

"Don't forget the stickers, we'll need to set up an account with one of the online stores for that," Roxy said from inside the shower.

"Yeah, but we'll need an artist first to do all the artwork."

"Oh, don't worry about that. I gotta friend. I'll call her when we're ready to leave here, and get the ball rolling."

"I'll probably need some graphics for the website too," Sean said, thinking about it. "Can I borrow your laptop and start laying it out?"

"After we eat!" Jolene warned.

"Yes, after we eat," Sean agreed.

"So when are we heading back to Reno?" Roxy asked.

"Tomorrow," Sean said and yawned, if he wasn't so hungry, he'd just go back to bed. "Right now they think I'm dead, so we have a breather. If something big is supposed to happen on my birthday, well, they'll know I'm not dead.

"Besides, Reno is probably the only place we'll be able to get online."

"Umm-hmmm. Too bad we don't have anything else to enchant!"

"I think I'm going to spend the night studying. There are a lot more spells I need to learn. Maybe something nice and offensive for a change."

Sean was sitting in his 'classroom' and he was digging through the books. He'd pushed a few more points into enchanting spells; because he wanted to be sure he had that completely understood. He knew now that any magic item he held, he could easily just make a tarball of, and then play it back into another, similar object. Eventually he'd rewrite that spell so that the object didn't have to be the same, but right now, it was good enough.

The thing he wanted to do next was figure out just how to put his firewall spell into an object, like a coin or a ring, so he could then give it to Roxy. That was turning out to be just a little more complicated than he expected, but not because it was difficult, but because the way his firewall spell worked wasn't typical for an enchanted item.

Once he'd finally figured out just *how* to do it, Sean moved on to shield spells. He wanted ones to protect him from spells cast on him, like the paralysis spell that had been used, or some of the attack spells that had been cast at him. He found and learned spells to protect against magical fire, magical cold, and the like, but it wasn't until he was too sleepy to continue that he realized the spells like paralyze and sleep were mind attack spells, not manifestations of physical elements, and were in a completely different book.

Checking his stats before calling it quits for the night he saw that his strength had gone up a little more and that he'd gained another point there, surprisingly. He pushed them all into regeneration, because almost dying had scared the hell out of him.

Mental he was very surprised to notice that both his Intelligence and Wisdom had increased a little, but he was still out of points. In his magical abilities he'd gained four points and split them between Mana and Will. Having those go up would be helpful.

He'd already spent most of his points for spells tonight, and he figured he was finally getting the idea of just how this part worked. You had to dedicate your magical potential to specific fields of work as you matured. If you put it all into fire, you'd be better at fire and have an easier time learning fire type spells. Sean now had a lot of points into enchanting, which meant he had more magic and understanding available for enchanting.

However, because he'd cheated with his new idea 'framework' spells, it had actually created a new category on his 'character sheet', and it looked like whatever spell he cast using those frameworks would have the power of his framework magic behind it, and not say that of fire spells, which he'd only put a point in to be able to learn the basics.

All in all, it was still a little confusing, but he was finally starting to make sense of it.

Leaving the classroom, he let himself fall asleep. Tomorrow was another day after all.

Sean let Roxy drive them back to town while he sat there with one of his gold coins and started to enchant the firewall spell into it. He'd punched a hole through it, near the edge, so it could be worn with a chain or cord, the book on enchanting had been clear on two things, the first was that an object couldn't be physically altered *after* it was enchanted, or it would destroy the enchantment. The second was that those metals known as 'transition metals' were the only things that you could enchant, and the purer or more 'expensive' they were, the easier it typically was to enchant them. That made gold about the easiest to work with, so as this was his first effort, that was what he decided to start with.

For a spell that took Sean only a minute to cast on himself, it took him twenty minutes to cast it into coin. Some of that time was because he had to restart the process three times, as he realized he wasn't doing it properly. Once he was finished, he used his monitor program on it, which he could only do because he was holding it. He put in the same 'allow all' exceptions he had on his own, one for Roxy, one for Jolene, and of course, one for him.

Then pulling out another coin, he punched a hole in that one and did it all over again. This time it only took him a little more than ten minutes.

Setting the exceptions up on that one, he checked the results and then passed the first coin to Roxy.

"What's this?"

"It's the new protection from scrying spell I've worked out; Jo's using it now too. It's a lot better than the one I've been casting on you."

"How do I?"

"You can just put it in your pocket for now, but as long as it's on you, it'll work. We can get a chain or something for it later."

Roxy smiled, "Thanks, Hon! Now, let's hit the mall and replace some of those clothes you lost."

"And get me a new laptop as well, I guess," Sean agreed.

"I could use some clothes too," Jolene sighed. "I just wonder if it's safe to go back to my apartment?"

Sean shrugged, "Why take the chance? Let's drop by the post office, to mail these chains first, then yeah, shopping. After that, maybe some cash from the bank."

Sitting back in the seat while they drove through town, Sean made a tarball of the spell on the coin. It was a lot smaller than the one on the chain, and pulling out a third coin, he unpacked the tarball on to that. He got a little dizzy for a brief moment, from the magical surge, but again, most of the magic came back to him, it hadn't really used all that much. What he found interesting was that there was now a hole in the coin, just like the other one, even though he hadn't punched one. Also the exception files were there for him, Roxy, and Jolene as well.

Thinking back to the chains, he wondered how much harder would it be, if he was just casting the spell on to iron or steel ones? The finished products weren't gold or silver, or any single precious metal; they were obviously an alloy of several. So somehow he was transmuting a precious metal into a lot less precious combination of metals.

He'd have to find a physics book. Something about that just didn't seem exactly right.

Thursday Night

"Well, that's it," Sean sighed and closed his new laptop. "The new website is up, I've made the submittal for the go-fund-me page, and I just finished updating my social media pages. I even opened up an account with one of the online sticker companies; all we need now is the artwork."

Roxy nodded, "I got my friend working on it. She said she'll start having drawings in a week."

"So," Jolene asked, "now what?"

Sean sighed and rubbed his temples, they were sitting in a coffee shop using the wifi and he'd drunk way too much coffee. That along with the stress of everything was starting to get to him.

"I have no idea, tomorrow's my birthday and everyone thinks some sort of 'message' or something is going to be delivered to me by my father from beyond the grave or something."

"Maybe he sent you a telegram via western-union, you know, like in the movie?"

Sean shook his head, "Even if they still do that, which I doubt, how would they ever find me? Plus my dad was a magic user; I'd sort of expect him to use, oh, I don't know," Sean sighed, "*magic*?"

"Honestly, how do you even send a message to someone twelve years in the future?"

"Maybe it'll unlock on your birthday, like the books did?" Roxy suggested.

"Maybe, I donno, if this was my dad's biggest secret, I would think he'd want to do something to keep it from ever falling into the wrong people's hands."

"And there sure are a lot of those these days, aren't there?" Roxy agreed with a sigh.

"The most obvious method," Jolene said, in obvious thought, "would be to do something that would attract your attention to a specific place. So you'd go there."

"But then everyone would see it," Sean pointed out.

"True, but until the seers started seeing, you'd have been the only one to realize that it was for you, being *your* birthday and all. Plus whatever it does, it could easily be set to only activate when you came near."

"Makes sense," Roxy nodded.

"Yeah," Sean agreed, "it does, but what could you do to attract attention in Reno of all places? And without freaking out all the regular people?" Sean sighed again, "And of course, if that is what he did, then every magic user in town is gonna know what it's for, and we'll be dealing with that as well."

"Where did you live, before your father died?" Jolene asked.

"Down by Thomas Creek."

"Whoa, that's a pretty pricey neighborhood!"

Sean frowned, "We were rich. Until they took everything away that is. Why?"

"Well, if your father wanted to do something that you would see, don't you think he'd do it near where you lived?"

Roxy shook her head, "I think we're going about this all the wrong way. Sean, did you have a favorite place that your dad used to take you? Someplace that he knew you loved?"

"Well yeah, the railroad..." Sean stopped and looked at Roxy, "I remember now, how did I ever forget?"

"The geas," Jolene supplied.

"For my seventh and eighth birthdays, my dad took me to the railroad museum in Carson City. I loved that place! He knew some of the people rebuilding the old steam locomotives; we used to get tours of the workrooms in the back. I remember him telling me that it was one of his favorite places because of all the craftsmanship!"

"Sounds like that might be the place then," Roxy smiled.

"Well we better get going," Sean said and started to put all of his stuff away.

"What's the rush?"

"It's almost ten," Sean said and then looked at his watch a second time; he was surprised that they hadn't been kicked out yet! The looks on the faces of the two people behind the counter kind of made it clear that they wanted to close soon.

"It'll take about an hour to get there, and then we need to scope the place out, maybe find a place to stay, because for all I know, whatever is going to happen, may just happen at midnight."

"Yeah, let's get going," Roxy agreed and she and Jolene both got up and followed Sean to the exit.

"Oh, shit," Sean swore as he stepped out the door. There, across the parking lot, were four people, obviously waiting for them. Three of them looked to be in their mid-thirties, and definitely looked like they were only there to watch out for the fourth one, who looked much older. That one's hair was white, though short, and he had a goatee, also white. "Trouble," Sean growled in a low voice.

"Excuse me, Mr. Sean Valens, I presume?" The older man spoke up and took a step forward.

Sean activated his monitor spell to see if he was being scryed and reaching inside his vest, he put his hand on the butt of his pistol.

"I only wish to talk," the old man said and cast a spell at Sean.

Sean would have missed it if he hadn't had the monitor spell running; the gesture was so minor and discrete. The cast spell hit his firewall, and went nowhere.

"If you just want to talk, why are you casting at me?"

"Nothing more than a simple paralysis spell, it'll wear off shortly. I'd rather not be shot, you understand."

Sean stood there, unmoving for the moment, as he recalled that paralysis and sleep spells all affected the mind, but his firewall blocked those things rather effectively now.

That was an interesting side effect, and gave him some ideas for another spell. But first, he had to deal with this.

"Who are you, and what do you want?"

"I am Arthur Troy, I'm the current head of the local Council of Sapientia, and I must say that I'm a bit concerned over just what's been going on these last two weeks."

"*You're* concerned?" Sean boggled at him. "If you're so concerned, why aren't you going after the others? You know, the people who have tried to kidnap me, murder me, who've murdered my friend, kidnapped my mother, blew up my house and burned my apartment down?"

"Yes, well, I do regret all of that, but we had nothing to do with any of it."

"Then you have nothing to do with me either."

"Unfortunately, your actions do. You see, if you continue your father's work, it could lead to open conflict that would bring us all to the attention of the world at large. We simply can not have that. It would lead to many problems for all of us."

"Listen, old man," Sean growled. "I didn't start this, but I sure as hell am going to finish it, I no longer have any choice! It's win or die for me now, and I'm not all that fond of dying."

"You really do not want the Council of Sapientia as your opponents," Arthur warned, and Sean noticed him make another hand motion as another spell bounced off of his firewall. Sean made note of the spell 'object', he'd puzzle it out later.

"Wrong, it's you who need to be worried," Sean replied hotly, "because your spells won't work on me, and if you cast another one," Sean drew his pistol and pointed at the man, "you're going to be late."

"Late?" Arthur looked confused.

"As in the 'late Arthur Troy.' You've got ten seconds to get in your car, and leave."

"So, you can practice magic?" Arthur looked surprised.

"Again, not like I had any choice, so I suggest you don't force me to kill you and your men. Eight seconds."

Arthur sighed and turned back towards the car, "Jolene, please try to talk some sense into the boy," Arthur mentioned to the others, "Let's go."

"How'd you find us, Arthur?" Jolene called, "We're scry proof!"

"Oh really now, Jo, do you think I'm dumb?" Arthur got into the back of the car, as the others also got inside.

Sean watched as the car started up and slowly pulled out, Arthur lowering his window as they drove by.

"I put an alert on his credit card," Arthur smiled, "*old man* indeed."

Sean waited until they'd pulled out of the parking lot, then turned to Jolene, "He's?"

"My uncle," Jolene shrugged.

"What?"

"Magical ability is inherited, Hon, I thought you'd figured that out by now?"

"So everyone's related?"

Jolene shrugged, "Not directly, but if you go back far enough, I'm sure we've all got a common ancestor or three. Now I think we should split before anyone else shows up."

Sean nodded and they quickly went over to their car, "What was that second spell he cast?"

"Sleep spell. I think he was trying to show off a little."

"Well, that didn't work out for him, did it? Roxy, could you drive?"

"Sure, why?"

"I want to work on some more spells. I have an idea I want to try out."

Arthur sighed as they drove away; his niece had always been the wild card in the family. When it was discovered that her magic was too weak to follow in the family's traditions, it had broken his sister's heart. When Jolene had gone missing, everyone thought she'd just taken her life, to hide her family's shame.

Then three years later she'd come back, a tantric witch. And not just any tantric witch, oh no, his niece had somehow made her way to India and studied with the head of the tantric covens. She was sweeter, sexier, and from all reports a total seductress and rather accomplished in the bedroom.

Two marriages had quickly been destroyed by her. The women in them, Arthur had later found out, had been exceptionally abusive to Jolene before her disappearance. After that, to all appearances, she'd settled down at the local college, with a nice stable of boyfriends, some of whom Arthur suspected where respectable members of both his council as well as a few of the others.

While the rest of the family was now cool to her, Arthur had grown to respect his niece. She'd made the best of her situation and had come back to rub her success in the face of all those who had doubted her or slighted her. He always invited her to all of the family outings, and when she showed, he made sure to treat her like the rest of his nieces and nephews, and watched with quiet amusement as she baffled them all.

And now, to his surprise, he just discovered that she'd taken up with Ben Valens' son.

The whole Valens affair had been a rather messy one, and his niece had to have heard about it, she'd probably heard about her grandfather's role in it as well.

And yet, she'd sided with this Sean.

"James?"

"Yes, Boss?" James asked from the front seat, next to Dean, who was driving.

"I want to know everything about Sean Valens you can find. Where he lived, how much money he has in the bank, where he worked, where his mother worked, his high school and college records. All of that."

"Sure thing, Boss."

"You want me to follow them?" Charles, the guard sitting next to him asked.

Arthur nodded slowly. The last thing he wanted was for his niece to get hurt.

"Pull over when we're out of sight, Dean."

"Sure thing, Boss!"

Arthur turned to Charles, "Don't let them spot you, and don't do anything other than watch them. Find out what they're driving, where they're going. Don't try to get too close, and don't tell anyone who you're following or why. My niece sees something in this young man, and I want to know what it is before I try talking to him again."

"Okay, Boss."

Arthur sat in thought as the car pulled over and Charles got out, James had already called the backup car that had been waiting around the block to come and pick up Charles. He always kept an extra car nearby when conducting dangerous or clandestine meetings, just in case he needed someone followed, or needed to stop someone from following him.

Sean hunkered down into his classroom almost immediately and started on another feature to his firewall spell. Simply put, Sean created a honeypot trap that all blocked spells would go into and added a logging and an archiving function. All attacks would be logged, and the spell 'objects' that were now blocked by his firewall would be automatically 'tarred.' Next he added another feature that would allow him to 'play back' or actually cast those spells back immediately. The hard part was coming up with a naming convention, eventually he simply settled on the the number of which attack it was on that day. He'd have to make sure that he managed it well, so it didn't become a complete mess. But if nothing else, it would teach him more about how each person constructed their spells.

But the best part about the new 'archiving' function was that it drained the energy out of the spell as it was archived, so he'd gain energy from it. Which would definitely help if he was under attack, as shield spells were costly.

That made Sean wonder if he could attach the same function to his shield spell, but the more he looked at it, the more impossible it seemed. The objects became physical before they contacted the target, and the ability to convert physical objects into energy just wasn't possible it seemed.

Energy attacks were different, because energy could be manipulated, though from what he'd read so far it seemed that some forms of energy were harder to deal with than others. But in the cases of those attacks you were trying to overwhelm your victim's ability to deal with the energy being supplied. That wasn't easy against an experienced or trained magic user of course, so energy attacks, like lightning or heat were typically only used against mundanes or other non-magic wielding targets.

When Sean finally checked out of his classroom he found that they were parked in front of a motel in Carson City.

"Ah, back with us!" Roxy smiled and kissed him. "Jolene got us a room, and we moved some of our stuff in there.

"Well, I want to drive by the museum and get a look at it before tomorrow," Sean told her.

"We already did. It's closed. We made a lap around the parking lot, there were some lights on and a few cars, I guess someone was working there. But that was about it."

"I'd really like to go back there," Sean sighed.

"Well, it's only about a half mile south of us, so we could just walk on down there, but I'd rather wait until it's a lot later out, with less people around."

Sean nodded, "That sounds like a plan then, let's go inside."

Midnight at the Railroad

"Sean, wake up," Roxy was shaking his foot.

"What?" Sean opened his eyes, and sat up quickly.

"I think we have trouble," Roxy sighed.

Grabbing his pants, Sean started to get dressed. "What is it?"

"Look out the front window, carefully."

Grabbing his holster and putting it on, Sean walked over to the spot where Roxy had the shades propped open a little bit.

The parking lot looked fine, but there were a bunch of cars across the street, and as Sean watched someone came running across the street and started to check out their car.

"Jo, you don't think your uncle sold us out, do you?" Sean asked and grabbing his shirt he put it on and checking his watch he stepped into his shoes. It was a little past midnight; they'd been here about two hours.

"Him?" Jolene shook her head, "No. One of the men with him? Possibly."

"Well they at least they don't know what room we're in," Roxy said peeking out the window. "Uh-oh, one of them is running over to the front desk."

"Grab your packs," Sean said and went around to the back window, grabbing his as he did, and peeking out the shades.

"No one back here, yet. Jo, you wouldn't know any silence spells, would you?"

Jolene laughed, "With the way Rox moans? Of course I do!"

Roxy turned rather beat red as Sean grinned.

"You're not all that quiet yourself, you know. Could you cast it over here? I need to bust out this window so we can leave."

Jolene nodded and made a few gestures.

"Go for it," Jolene said.

Sean nodded and picking up the chair he quickly busted out the glass and framework of the window.

"I'll go through first, let's move."

"Yeah, the guy just came out of the office and is running back to the other guys," Roxy said.

Climbing out the window and being careful not to get cut, Sean helped Jolene out next and then Roxy. After that they took off down the street.

"So, they know we're here, now what?" Jolene asked.

"We go to the museum. It's after midnight, it's my birthday now. Maybe something will turn up."

"Happy birthday, Hon," Roxy sighed.

"Happy birthday," Jolene agreed as they ran, "I was sorta hoping we could have a little party."

Sean chuckled, "Oh, I'm sure we will, I'm just not sure when."

"Better pick up speed," Roxy murmured, and Sean noticed she had shifted into her hybrid form and was running a lot faster now. Shifting as well, Sean grabbed Jolene, and picking her up in a bridal carry he took off after Roxy.

"How long until they follow us?" Sean grunted.

"No idea," Roxy said as he caught up with her. "But I doubt it will take them all that long to figure it out. There's only two places we might be interested in, the State Museum to the north and the Railroad Museum to the south."

"Well, let's hope they check the one to the north first," Sean said as the came around the back of the museum.

"So, where do we start?" Jolene asked, looking around at the buildings as Sean set her back down.

"Let's start in the back," Sean said looking at the large building where the maintenance was done. "Odds are the front one with the fancier displays and the gift shop has an alarm."

"Well, let's be quick," Roxy said in a low voice.

Sean nodded and shifting back to make it easier to fit through the doorway, he grabbed the doorknob on the first door he came to, and carefully forced the lock using his strength. He winced as the lock mechanism shattered, it wasn't too loud, but it still wasn't quiet.

"I just wish I knew what we were looking for," Sean grumbled and slowly led them inside the building. It was dark inside, but that didn't present much of a challenge for Sean anymore, or Roxy, and Jolene just cast some sort of spell to see in the darkness as they started searching.

"You know, if it's going to be anyplace, it's going to be in the front building," Roxy sighed as they slowly made their way back towards the workshops. "Everything here just moves around too much."

"Still, my dad was a fan of the workshops, so we need to check them out," Sean whispered.

"At least the place is empty," Jolene said looking around.

Sean looked around and nodded, and suddenly remembered being here with his father so many years ago. Following the route of his memory, sure enough, they came to the door to the workshop, along with a sign about authorized personnel only.

Opening the door he stepped through, surprisingly a lot of it looked just like his memory of the place.

Except of course for the small woman in coveralls standing in the middle of the room with a fairly large hammer in her right hand.

"Umm, Hello?" Sean said.

"Who are you, an' just what are you doing in my shop?"

"Your shop?" Sean gave a laugh, looking around. "I seem to recall an old guy running this place. Samis, something? Heavyset man, black and gray beard?"

"Yeah, that's my uncle. Now, I suggest you turn around and leave while you still can!"

Sean looked her over, she was young, probably his age, and had to be all of five feet, if that. She really wasn't that big, or wasn't that strong obviously.

Sean raised a hand, "Chill, I'm looking for something my dad left for me. He was a friend of your uncle's."

"Look, I ain't got no time for tweakers looking for stuff to steal to buy drugs. I suggest you leave now, before I take this hammer and start breaking yer bones!"

Sean rolled his eyes, "Yeah, you and what army. Listen I'm not here to steal anything. Just let me see if I can find this thing, then I'll get the hell out of here."

"What, you don't think I can take ya' down?" She said, scowling at Sean, and started to smack the hammer into her left hand.

"Umm, Sean," Roxy started.

"Are you suicidal?" Sean said staring at the woman, "I'm bigger, taller, and obviously just a little bit desperate, being in here this late at night. You're just a single small woman and you don't even have a gun! No, you can't take me down! God, why do I have to run into the crazy ones all the time!"

Sean stepped into the room, walking over towards where a part of what he guessed was a steam engine was sitting on a worktable, with tools racked on the wall behind it, and the crazy gal actually threw the hammer at him!

It hit him in the chest, and he was sure he felt a rib crack as he grunted.

"Sean!" Roxy said again, "She's a dwarf!"

"Huh?" Sean blinked as the hammer rather amazingly returned to the young woman's hand. "Dwarves are real?" and then he ducked as she threw it at his head this time, just missing him, but it clipped him on the back of the head as it came back.

"So," she smiled at him, "still think I need an army?"

"Oh, fuck this!" Sean growled and shifted. "I've had about enough of this shit for today!" and stepped towards her.

Sean noticed her eyes got a little wider, and she took a step back, but it didn't stop her from throwing her hammer at him a third time.

Jumping her, he wrestled her down to the ground and then rolled over rather quickly as he figured that hammer was coming back to hit him again.

Sure enough, it was, but she caught it as he dodged it and swung it at him, as they struggled. He was rather amazed at how strong she was, definitely not as strong as a young woman should be! But also not as strong as he was. She caught him in the side of the face with the hammer and it spun his head to the side, lighting up with a fire that wasn't natural. Grabbing her hand he pinned it to the ground hard and putting his other hand around her throat he pinned her to the floor.

"I think the damn thing is silver," Sean growled, he could feel the blood flowing down the side of his face. The wound wasn't healing.

"Let me see," Roxy said and running over she checked the side of his muzzle.

"Quit struggling," Sean growled down at the woman under him, "you like getting hurt or something?"

"Yeah, that hammer's got silver in it, quite a lot. Jo, you got any healing spells?"

Jolene came over, skirting the struggling woman under Sean and put her hand on his head, a warm pleasant feeling surged through him, at the same time he felt the woman digging her fingers of her free hand into the pressure points of his elbow.

Looking down at her, he growled. "Stop that."

"She's not going to stop fighting you, Sean," Roxy sighed. "They're like that."

"How long until my face heals?" Sean asked Jolene.

"Oh, twelve hours or so I'd guess?"

"What?"

"Silver really messes up lycans, Sean," Roxy sighed. "At least it'll heal. Now, what are we going to do about her?"

Grumbling Sean looked down at the dwarven woman beneath him. This close he could see that she was really quite cute, no strike that, beautiful was more like it, even with the murder in her eyes as she glared up at him. The body inside that coverall, that he was now sitting on top of, also appeared to be a lot nice than he'd guessed.

"My name is Sean," he sighed, looking down at her, "Sean Valens. You are?"

"Daelyn Goldsmith, and I'm going to kill your furry ass!"

Sean took a deep breath and shook his head. "Look, my father was murdered twelve years ago and he left me something that I need to find, today, on my twenty-first birthday. This was one of our favorite places to come when I was a kid; he was friends with the people who worked here, so I'm hoping this is where he hid it.

"Now, there are a butt load of people trying to kill me because of who my father was. So if you want a piece of me, you'll just have to wait in line, okay? But right now, I need to get into the main building, and as I see it, you probably have the keys and the alarm code."

"And just why would I help *you?*"

"Because I don't want to damage anything?"

"Daelyn," Roxy said, coming over to kneel by Daelyn's head. "If we go in there and set off the alarm, about a dozen people who want him dead and who are looking for us right now will come here."

"So?"

"They're magic users with nasty weapons. What do you think will happen to this place?"

Daelyn gave Roxy an evil look.

"We have gold," Roxy said with a smile.

"Like that'll make me change my mind!" Daelyn said.

"How about this," Sean growled, "after we go through the main building, if we find what we want, you can take us *and* it to your uncle's house and he can decide if I get to keep it or not?"

"And the gold?"

"I've got six ounces left that I haven't enchanted, you can have them all."

"Wait, you can enchant gold?" Daelyn's eyes did get wide, "Lycan's can't enchant things!"

"Yeah, well, this one can," Roxy chuckled. "So, deal or no deal?"

"And if I say no?"

"I'll tie you up and trash your tool bench," Sean growled.

"Okay, you got my word, I won't attack you and I'll let you into the main building. *But* we go to my uncle's afterwards, regardless. Okay?"

"Deal," Sean sighed and sat back on his heels, letting go of Daelyn and touching the side of his muzzle gingerly with his left hand.

"Well, at least the bleeding's stopped," he sighed and shifted back to human form, then gasped in pain.

"Oh, yeah, shifting when you're wounded hurts, I should have warned you." Roxy apologized, looking a little embarrassed.

"Never mind, let's just go."

"Man, I got you good, didn't I?" Daelyn laughed looking at Sean.

"I thought dwarves were supposed to be short, wide, and have beards," Sean grumbled back at her.

"That's the men," Roxy said, "though I don't remember ever meeting a dwarven girl as tall as you are, Daelyn."

"If you start telling tall jokes, I'll introduce ya' to Maxwell here, like I did yer boyfriend!"

"Tall jokes?" Sean blinked, "You're not tall!"

Daelyn glared at Sean, who looked confused.

Roxy facepalmed, "You named your hammer Maxwell?"

"Yeah, well, he's silver," Daelyn said looking back at Roxy. "What else would you name him?"

Sean looked at Daelyn and decided right now keeping his mouth shut was a good idea.

"Let's go," he said and pointed to the exit.

"So, why are you here tonight, anyway?" Sean asked as they crunched across the gravel to the back door of the museum.

"Thursday and Friday are my off days from work, so I came down here to help with an old brass steam coupling valve set." Daelyn sighed, "They don't make 'em like that anymore, kinda surprising at times that humans were ever able to make 'em in the first place. Anyways, I lost track of the time, and just decided to sack out in the shop instead of going home."

"Work? What'ya do?"

"Slot machine maintenance, primarily the old mechanical ones, though I'll work on the new ones too." Daelyn shook her head and Sean suddenly noticed the thick braid of hair that went down her back and past her butt, "The new ones aren't as much fun to fix though. Too easy."

Taking out a key ring, Daelyn unlocked the back door, then stepping inside she keyed a panel by the door with a code.

"Okay, we got thirty minutes, then the alarm'll come back on. That's the bathroom break code. If I enter it a second time, people will come."

Sean nodded, "I don't think it'll take that long. Whatever my father left, I suspect it'll react when I walk by.

"Fine, let's just be quick. Follow me," Daelyn grumbled and Sean did just that, though he found it a little hard to keep his eyes off her butt as she walked. She really had a nice one he was starting to realize. Sean also quickly realized that she wasn't wearing anything at all under those coveralls.

"Are you watching my butt?" Daelyn sighed, glancing back over her shoulder at him.

"What guy could resist?" Sean teased with a grin, and then started looking at the exhibits around him.

"Wow, this place is smaller than I remembered it."

"You were eight the last time you were here," Jolene laughed, "of course it is."

"Better hurry up," Roxy said over from the front door as they walked around the place, which she was looking through.

"Trouble?"

"Yeah, one of the cars we saw back at the motel is cruising the lot."

"Well," Daelyn said a minute later, "we've covered all of it, and nothing's happened."

"You sure?" Sean said looking around. "This has to be the place!"

"You sure it isn't over at the V and T?"

"The Vee and Tee?" Sean asked.

"Virginia and Truckee Railroad, they run steam engines and put on a show."

Sean shook his head slowly, "I don't really recall that. Maybe we should look again?"

Daelyn shook her hammer at him, "We looked, nothing happened; now unless you want Max upside your head again, we're done here."

"Sean," Jolene said, "nothing happened, or I would have felt it. We need to go, before the others show up and we end up having to fight our way out."

"Too late for that," Roxy said coming around to them, "the other car just got here and they're all getting out and spreading out.

"Well, shit!" Daelyn swore.

Sean fished out the pouch in his pocket with the gold pieces in it and tossed it to Daelyn, "Catch!"

"What's this?"

"The gold I promised. No reason for you to get involved in this, not your fight." Sean looked at Jolene and Roxy, "Let's head west up into the hills, draw them away from here."

Running for the back door, Sean hit it, pistol in hand with Jolene behind him and Roxy bringing up the rear.

"There they are!" Sean heard someone yell and grabbing Jolene he ducked around behind a train as Roxy sprinted by.

Sean waited, and sure enough, two men went running by, hot on Roxy's heels. He grabbed the first one by the hair and dragging him backwards as his feet flew out from under him, Sean brought the base of the gun down hard on the man's head, knocking him out.

Jolene meanwhile cast some sort of spell and the other guy just suddenly locked up stiff as a board as his clothing suddenly shrank tight enough to leave him whimpering in pain on the ground.

"Kinky," Sean whispered and peeking around the corner he saw six more men running their way.

"Run, I'll catch up," Sean said and gave Jolene a push. Then calling up his monitor spell and his offense framework he fired off a fireball and then winced as it went off with a rather loud 'boom' and the six men dove for cover. That rattled the windows and no doubt set off any alarms in the area.

Turning, Sean took off in the direction of Jolene and passed Roxy, who was taking cover behind a rise that had a few trees on it.

Stopping and turning back to join her Sean hunkered down.

"Well, we took two of them out, how many do you think are left?"

"At least ten, I'm sure," Roxy said. "Keep your eyes open for any flanking actions."

Sean nodded and looked down his pistol sights as a group of men came running around the corner. Both he and Roxy opened up at the same time, dropping the front two as the rest all dove for cover and returned fire.

"Four down," Sean said and cast a shield spell on Roxy, and them himself.

"That leaves six," Roxy agreed as they heard the sound of squealing tires in the distance.

"Great, now they're gonna throw cars at us," Sean grumbled.

"I'm surprised they're not throwing spells at us."

Sean checked his monitor spell, and saw that he'd had over a dozen spells thrown at him.

"Actually, they have been," Sean said and with a series of gestures he threw the last six spells throw at him back at the group shooting at them.

"That do any good?" Sean asked ducking back down into cover.

"No idea, and that car is getting closer."

"Go protect Jo, I'll catch up with both of you in a minute," Sean said and popped a couple more shots off at the guys on the ground.

"Don't take too long," Roxy said and streaked out of there.

Sean nodded and watched as a man came running around the corner and started to charge straight at him. Taking aim, Sean, double tapped him, in the body, but he kept coming, so Sean hit him in the thigh, where he was sure there wasn't any body armor.

The guy stumbled, but kept coming. Swearing, Sean stood up and quickly moved his now empty pistol to his left hand and punched the guy in the face.

The guy stopped and looked at Sean, and then slowly grinned, "Not bad, but now it's my turn!" and hauling off he hit Sean in the head as well, causing Sean to curse in pain as he hit the damaged spot on the side of his face.

"Give it up boy, you can't win against me!" the man growled.

Sean kicked him hard in the balls and then head butted him as the man howled in pain.

"The hard way then," the man growled and as Sean watched, he shifted, and suddenly Sean was facing a seven-foot-tall werewolf.

Dropping his pistol Sean shifted as well, roaring in pain from the wound on his face and anger that some dog would even think it could stand up to him! Lunging at the now shorter wolf, they both started to hit and tear at each other, but the look of both shock and surprise on the werewolf's face as he suddenly found himself facing down a much bigger and stronger werelion was clear.

"It can't be!" the werewolf growled, "You can't be one of us!"

Sean hit him hard in the chest, pushing him back, and in the space of that moment he cast another fireball back at the men who had started to shoot at them again just as the werewolf in front of him screamed in agony, and grabbed at his side as a bullet passed through his body and just barely missed Sean.

"Nice people you work for there," Sean growled and grabbed him.

"I have no choice," the werewolf snarled and tried to fight Sean off as Sean grabbed him by the throat and the belt around his waist.

"Yeah, I've been hearing that a lot lately," Sean said and picking up the werewolf he threw him back at the others who were still sorting themselves out from the fireball. Scooping up his pistol he ran off towards Roxy, who was now calling his name, changing magazines on his pistol for another full one as he did.

Passing over the railroad tracks he saw Roxy was waving to him by an old muscle car with what looked like racing slicks, which she dove into as soon as he turned towards her. Vaulting over the hood of the car, Sean shifted and jumped into the passenger's seat. Sitting in the driver's seat was Daelyn, who floored the car, driving Sean back into his seat as the door slammed closed and with a loud roar the car took off.

"What the hell is this thing?" Sean gasped.

"Nineteen-Seventy Hemi 'Cuda, last of the big muscle cars," Daelyn laughed. "Like it? We're already doing a hundred and fifty! There ain't nothing that can catch this car!"

Sean looked up and out the window of the old car as Daelyn slid them around a slight curve with a downshift and then slamming on the brakes cut them into a parking lot, where she punched it again, as they screamed by a lamp post with inches to spare and then out onto the main road where if he'd thought they were going fast before, the dotted lines now looked like a solid bar.

"Are you trying to get the police on our tail?" Sean yelled, his fingers sinking into the dashboard as he held on for dear life.

"Car's enchanted," Daelyn laughed, "they can hear it, but they can't see it and best of all," Daelyn turned and smiled at him, "no radar!"

Swearing Sean looked at the girls in the back seat. Jolene had her eyes closed tight and appeared to be praying. Roxy had her eyes wide open and was laughing and bouncing up and down in the seat.

"Better put your seatbelt on," Daelyn told him, "the corners are a bit rough at one sixty."

Sean put on the lap belt and then tried to figure out the archaic, shoulder belt.

"Just where the hell are we going?" he asked.

"My uncle's, remember?"

"What about the guys back there?"

"Oh, me and Max took care of them. I don't think they're gonna be in any kind of shape to remember me none," Daelyn laughed.

'I think I'm in love,' Sean's lion suddenly piped up.

'She's an insane maniac!' Sean pointed out.

'And Roxy isn't?'

Sighing Sean sank back in the seat and had to admit, once the fear had worn off, that Daelyn sure as hell could drive.

"Are all dwarves as crazy as you?" Sean asked as they whipped around a pair of cars by using the shoulder. He was amazed at how Daelyn kept the car from even slowing down as they hit the gravel.

"Nah, the men are far worse!"

They turned a hard right then and went barreling down another road.

"Just how far is his place?" Sean asked, holding on as Daelyn suddenly dropped two gears and navigated a series of intersections and s-turns then turned onto a road skirting a hill.

"Right about," she locked up the car and did a four wheel drift around a corner and they ended up facing a garage door that was already opening, "here!"

"Wow! That was fun! Can we do that again!" Roxy laughed from the back, "Next time I'm sitting up front!"

Daelyn looked at Sean, "She's a cheetah, isn't she?"

Sean nodded, "How'd you know?"

"Eh, they're all speed freaks."

"Hey! It's not often I get to ride in something faster than me!" Roxy laughed from the back.

"She's got a point there," Sean said with a heavy sigh. "You still with us Jo?"

"We've stopped, right?"

"Yes, and the engine is even off," Daelyn said and shut the car off as they rolled into the garage and stopped.

"Then yes, I am still with you. I think, however, that my stomach is still a few miles behind us."

"Eh, it'll catch up. Come on," Daelyn opened her door and got out, "time to meet the family."

Sean got out of the car, and helped Roxy, then quickly went around and offered his support to Jolene, who obviously was not all that enamored with going fast, or Daelyn's driving.

"I didn't see a house," Sean said thinking back to the view around the garage as they'd slid to a stop. There was what looked like a large metal shed, and not much else.

"Course not, we live in a mountain, we're dwarves, why would we live in houses?"

Sean shrugged, "Up until an hour ago dwarves were just something from fantasy for me. So I didn't want to presume."

Daelyn stopped and turned and looked at him. "You mean to tell me that you, a werelion, have never heard of dwarves before?"

"You have to forgive him," Roxy snickered, "up until a couple of weeks ago, he hadn't even heard of werelions."

"How did that happen?" Daelyn looked at Sean curiously.

"I got bit," Sean said and then shrugged, "it's a long story, how about we go meet your uncle first?"

"Sure, come on," Daelyn and led them into a back room and closing the door she did something and suddenly the floor started to descend.

"Elevator?" Jolene said looking around.

"Yeah, easier to hide than a staircase."

After a hundred feet or so, it slowed and then stopped. There was a door in one of the walls now and pushing it open, Daelyn led the way.

"Hey, Dae!" A short but very strong looking young man said, jogging up to them, "You can't just bring people down here!"

Daelyn made a rude noise at him, "Two lycans and a magic user, Jocco. They're here to see Samis. Like I'd bring a regular human down here."

"Oh, I thought maybe you had a hot date or something," Jocco laughed.

Sean noticed Daelyn winced at that, so stepping forward he grabbed Jocco by the neck and picked him up off the floor.

"That was rather rude of you," Sean growled as Jocco grabbed at his wrist with both hands and tried to free himself.

"Oh, yeah," Daelyn chuckled, "my friend here is a lion *and* a magic user with a bit of an attitude problem. Plus I think he kinda likes me.

"Put him down, Sean."

"Do I have to?" Sean grumbled.

"He's my cousin, so yeah, you kinda have to."

Sean sighed and opened his hand, dropping Jocco, who landed on his feet and glared angrily at Sean a moment and then stomped off.

"Come on, let's go see my uncle," Daelyn said shaking her head and led them off down the same corridor Jocco had just gone down.

Sean took a moment to look around as they went. The walls of the elevator shaft had looked like concrete, same for the walls of the room they'd stepped out into, which had several exits from it. But the hallway they were in now was much of a more 'homey' feeling. The walls were smooth and painted, and there were occasional pictures or designs along it. The lighting was indirect; Sean wasn't quite sure what type of lighting it was.

At the end of the hallway, they came to another hallway that went off to either side and which had doors spaced randomly along it. Daelyn turned left down that hallway, and after about ten doors she stopped and knocked on it.

"Come on in, Daelyn." A man's voice called.

"I guess Jocco got here first," Daelyn sighed.

Opening the door and leading them in, Sean took in the rather large room with the surprisingly high ceiling. The room was obviously some sort of family room or den, he could see what looked like a kitchen off to one side, and two hallways led away from the back wall. There were several men and women in it as well. The men were all well under six-foot, two of them were barely five-foot tall. But they were all strongly built, and with the exception of Jocco and one other, they all had beards, though they were keep short and rather neat.

The women in the room were all, simply put, gorgeous. They all had their hair worn long, as Daelyn did, and while some of them were a bit heavier built that Daelyn, it didn't subtract from their beauty one bit. Sean also noticed that none of them were as tall as Daelyn was. They weren't even close.

"So, what's this I hear about you strangling my son?" The man standing next to Jocco said. Sean stopped and leaning forward a little he stared at the man, his hair was a little shorter now, and Sean could definitely see a lot more gray at the temples and even a few strands of it in his beard.

"Samis?" Sean said.

"Yeah, that's me. Now just what were you doing to my boy here?"

"Wow," Sean said, "you still look the same! I can't believe it! I had no idea you were a dwarf! Dad never told me!"

Samis rolled his eyes, "Do I know you, boy?"

"Sean Valens, my father, back before he was murdered, used to bring me down to see your shop and the trains," Sean smiled and stuck out his hand.

"You're Ben's kid?" Samis said and squinted at him a moment, "Damn, son, when did you get to be so big?" Stepping up he took Sean's hand and shook it. "Sorry about what happened to your father, he was a good man. Not all stuck up and stuff like most of the casters and enchanters these days."

"Dad!" Jocco said.

Samis rolled his eyes, "Oh yeah, my son. What did he do this time?"

"He insulted Daelyn," Sean grumbled, "I mean cousin or no, you don't go insulting people in front of guests, especially not me," Sean blushed a little as he said that.

"Sampson bit him," Roxy piped up.

"Who's Sampson?" Daelyn said.

"Why'd he do a thing like that?" Samis asked.

"It's a long story," Sean gave a little sigh, "but I'd be more than happy to tell it to you."

"Dad!" Jocco grumbled.

Samis turned to his son, "Jocco, I've warned you before to mind your tongue in front of strangers. Lions, especially young ones, can be a bit touchy if you go insulting the women they're with. Now go bring up a keg for our guests, and make sure you grab the good stuff."

Samis turned back to Sean then, "He's still learning, now, would you mind introducing me to your friends?"

Sean introduced Roxy and Jolene, and Samis then introduced his wife, Sarah, his other son, his three daughters, the husbands of two of them and the fiancé of the third, and his two friends Robert and Wilhelm.

They were then shown to some rather nice seats as Jocco carried a good-sized metal keg into the kitchen, and Sarah and her three daughters went into the kitchen as well, and returned a minute later with filled mugs and started serving everyone.

"Well, now that we have something to drink, why don't you tell me your story, Sean?"

Sean nodded, "How much do you know about my father's murder, if you don't mind my asking?"

"I knew his death was suspicious, but beyond that, very little. Your father had made some very powerful enemies, and I don't think he even realized it, until it was too late."

Sean took a drink of his beer, eyebrows rising at the taste, it was better than anything he'd ever had before.

"Well, I guess I'll start at the beginning and tell you everything I know," and starting back from the attempted kidnapping on Friday, two weeks ago, Sean told him the story of what he'd been through.

An hour later, when Sean had finally finished he looked up at Samis, who was sitting there with his head propped up by his left hand, his left elbow resting on his left knee, obviously deep in thought.

After a minute he nodded slowly, "A lot's been going on, but it's late, very late. I got a guest room in the back you can all sleep in. In the morning we can talk about this some more. Until then, feel free to enjoy my hospitality." Samis turned to Daelyn who was looking rather tired. Jolene had already fallen asleep, even Roxy looked tired.

"Dae, show them the guest room, and help them get settled in."

Standing up and stretching, Dae nodded, "Yes, Uncle."

"And for the love of stone and earth, put on some nice clothes when you come back in the morning, understand me?"

Daelyn blushed and nodded, "Yes, Uncle."

Yawning, Sean stood up and stretched, "Thank you, Samis, very much. I'm in your debt."

"Think nothing of it, Sean. Your father was one of the few humans and the only caster I ever called friend."

Sean nodded and bending over he picked up Jolene and carrying her, still sleeping form, he followed Roxy and Daelyn down one of the halls to a rather nice room with a very large bed, and its own bathroom and shower.

Setting Jolene down on the bed, Sean went over and bending slightly he pulled a rather surprised Daelyn into a hug.

"What's that for?" she protested, squirming and pushing back at him.

"For saving our lives," Sean smiled, "and I wanted to get an idea of just what you're hiding under those coveralls!"

Daelyn blushed rather heavily and turning left the room after Sean let go of her, closing the door behind her.

"Already lining up another one?" Roxy snickered.

Sean felt his face flush in embarrassment, "I can't help it. My lion's already in love with her."

"Uh-huh," Roxy teased and started to strip her clothes off, "and you're not?"

"I don't know," Sean said a little exasperated, "yeah she's hot, and tough, and as crazy as the rest of us. But a third wife?" Sean threw his hands up in the air, "Two weeks ago I was a virgin, now I have two incredibly wonderful and beautiful mates and yet I'm looking at lining up a third? How does this even happen?"

Roxy came over to him and started helping him undress.

"It's a lion thing," she giggled and kissed him on the mouth, and then slowly started to work her way down his neck, and then his chest, as she undid his belt.

"And you're okay with it?" Sean asked, watching as she pulled his pants down and started to rub her face against his already stiff tool.

"I knew what I was getting into when I brought you back to my room, Hon," Roxy said and then ran her tongue up his length, making his whole body shiver.

"And now, that you're in it?" Sean gasped, and reaching down he put his hands on her head, steadying him.

"I love you, Sean. I'm not human, neither are you anymore. Accept it. It's just the way lions are and everyone knows it."

"Everyone?" Sean blinked.

"Including Daelyn, *and* her uncle," Roxy laughed softly and took him into her mouth, and Sean decided that any further conversation could wait until morning.

"A moment, Dae," Samis said, following his niece out into the hallway.

"What?" Daelyn said stopping and looking up at him.

"I want you to dress up tomorrow, put on your finest dress, unbraid your hair; I want you to be beautiful, to show off the looks that you inherited from your mother, my sister."

Daelyn scowled at her uncle, "And why would I do that?"

"You'll do it because I asked you to, that's why," Samis said looking down at her, and then sighed, "Dae, have I not been like a father to you, since your parents died? Have I not looked out for you at every moment? Have I not been there for you when you needed it? Given you help, advice and guidance as if you were my very own child?"

Daelyn sighed, "Yes Uncle Samis, I'm sorry, I'll dress up for him tomorrow."

"Don't just do it for him, Dae, do it for *you!* Do it for yourself! He's interested in you, can't you see that?"

"But he's not a dwarf!" Daelyn protested.

"So? Do you really think that you're going to find a husband still? You're almost twenty-two and not a single man has paid court to you, ever. It has hurt me greatly to see you so ignored, especially when you're so bright and talented and easily as beautiful as my sister was."

Daelyn felt her eyes start to water; it hurt to hear her uncle say it, those things that had been whispered behind her back for so many years now. Turning away from him, she hid her face.

Samis grabbed his niece and turned her back to face him, "He comes from a family that has been friends with ours for generations. He has the power of magic and it is strong inside him, and he is a lion. He has already taken two mates of great power, and now his eye has fallen on you.

"Don't spurn him, Daelyn, don't turn him down out of hand. Lions are picky when it comes to those that they court, trust me that his attentions to you will not go unnoticed. Others will start to wonder what they have missed."

"So, you're saying I should just lead him on, so that others will change their minds about me?"

"No, I'm saying that you should give him a chance to be your man. No one will look down on you if you join his pride, and become his woman. Lions are respected, you know that."

"And he'll beat up anyone who disrespects me," Daelyn said with a sniffle.

"What man won't for the woman he loves?" Samis agreed, "But the point I'm trying to make is don't turn him down because he's not a dwarf, don't be afraid that letting him court you will make your life worse.

"And most importantly, don't be afraid to say yes if this is the male that will make you happy. Besides," Samis grinned, "he needs you. Really, I'd of thought that'd be obvious even to you!"

Daelyn laughed and wiped her eyes. "Yeah, you're right about that! He's still so clueless on so many things! I can see that Roxy and Jo are trying, but they definitely need help."

She hugged her uncle then, "Thank you, Uncle Samis. You're right as always."

Samis smiled and hugged his niece back, and then watched as she headed back to her home, she'd inherited her family's abode when her parents had died in an unfortunate accident so many years ago. Her only brother had found a wife and a job in another community, so she lived alone now. While her skill with machines, as well as that hammer of hers, were quite admired by all, her height still kept the suitors at bay.

Daelyn thought about what her uncle had said. When Sean had put Jocco in his place for insulting her, a nice warm feeling had gone through her, no man had ever done that for her before.

And then that hug! That boy had some serious muscle on him! And honestly? The idea of a man who was way bigger than her? Stronger than her? Oh yeah, she liked that idea alright, because until tonight she'd never met the man who was.

Happy Birthday

Two things quickly registered on Sean's mind, when he finally stumbled out of the room in the morning, still somewhat tired. After Roxy had finished with him last night, Jolene had woken up and started in.

The first was that they were having a birthday party for him.

The second was that with her hair undone and wearing a nice dress, Daelyn had a body that any man would kill for.

He just stood there, staring at her. There was definitely something to be said about short girls.

Daelyn blushed after a moment, and then scowled at him.

"Don't go getting any ideas, buster!"

Sean smiled and shook his head slowly, "Too late for that!" He motioned towards the tables that were being set up in the living room, "Is that what I think it is?"

Daelyn suddenly smiled, which made her look even more radiant, and nodded. Sean got the feeling she could make his lion sit up and beg.

"Twenty-one is when you come of age in dwarven society, and my uncle said it wouldn't be fair to let it go uncelebrated, especially after all you've lost."

Sean blinked, "Really?"

"Your father was a *really* good friend of my uncle's," Daelyn sighed and shook her head.

Sean frowned, "And that makes you sad, why?"

Daelyn held out the sack with the gold coins Sean had given her.

"It means I can't take this," and she handed it back to him.

"Are you sure?" Sean said and looked into the small sack. The six unmagicked coins, as well as the four now enchanted ones were still there.

"You can't pay friends for helping you," Daelyn told him. "It's one of our older customs. You help friends and family for free, because you can't set a price on their bonds and loyalty."

Sean nodded slowly, and took one of the enchanted coins out of the sack, which he then held it out to her as he slipped the rest into his pocket.

"I'd like you to take this, as a gift."

Daelyn rolled her eyes, "I just told you I can't."

Sean smiled, "This isn't one of the gold pieces I offered to pay you. This is an enchanted gold medallion, and I'd like you to wear it. I think it would look good on you."

Sean was rewarded with Daelyn blushing all the way down into her cleavage, which was easily as big as Jolene's, which made it rather impressive, as Daelyn was half a foot shorter.

"You want me to wear it?"

Sean nodded and smiled as she took it, suddenly looking rather shy.

"What does it do?" Daelyn asked, turning it over and looking at it.

"It protects you from scrying and mind based spells, like sleep or paralyze."

"Oh!" Daelyn paused a moment, "Do Roxy and Jolene have them?"

"Roxy does, but Jolene's a magic user, so I just taught her the spell."

"Thank... thank you," Daelyn said softly and blushed again. "I think I'll go find a nice chain to wear it on. Excuse me for a few minutes.

"Of course," Sean said and then opened his eyes wide as Daelyn stepped forward and gave him a rather warm hug, then quickly left the room.

Looking up, Sean saw Samis and his wife Sarah smiling.

"I didn't do anything wrong, did I?" Sean asked

"No, son, nothing wrong at all," Samis said with a chuckle.

"Come," Sarah said and beckoned him to the kitchen, "let's get some food into you before the party starts! Samis, why don't you go knock on the door and see if the others are awake yet?"

Sean followed Sarah into the kitchen and was rather amazed at the amount of food she set in front of him, not that he complained! He started in on it with a will as he was starving.

"I always love a man with a good appetite!" Sarah laughed.

"Thanks," Sean said, between bites. After a few minutes he paused, "May I ask something about Daelyn?"

Sarah nodded, "Of course, Sean. What would you like to know?"

"I'm kinda getting the impression that she's not all that popular with the guys, and considering her looks, which please, don't take this the wrong way, are a lot better than any of the girls I've met down here, and well, *why?* I'd expect there to be a long line of men after her."

Sarah sighed, "It's her height. Daelyn's a good six inches taller than most girls. Why she's as tall as or taller than many men."

"So?"

"Dwarven men don't like tall women much, Sean."

Sean blinked, "That has to be the stupidest thing that I've ever heard."

"Knowing her as well as I do, I'd be inclined to agree with you on that, Sean." Sarah nodded, and then added with a wink, "But their loss is your gain, right?"

Sean felt his lion actually sit up and pay attention. Sarah was smiling at him very warmly.

"I'm not a dwarf," Sean replied slowly as his mind happily considered that thought. Of course his lion was now pushing the idea, and honestly Sean had no intentions of resisting.

"Ah, but your family is good friends with a number of dwarves, it wasn't just your father, but his father, and his father too. Plus, you're not human, you're a lion."

"Why does everyone keep telling me that being a lion makes things different?"

"Because they're one of the few lycans that take non-lycans as wives. In every race, there is the one group that is the exception to the usual rules, and for lycans, that's the lions."

"So, it wouldn't reflect badly on Daelyn if I were to pursue her?" Sean said with a smile as Roxy and Jolene, fresh out of the shower entered the kitchen, yawning.

"Oh no, in fact it would be quite welcomed," Sarah turned to the girls as they entered and pointed them at seats, then started to heap a large amount of food on a plate which she gave to Roxy, who started in on it with a single minded intensity. Jolene's plate was somewhat less filled, but she started in on hers almost as quickly.

"So, they trying to set you up with Daelyn yet?" Roxy whispered to him.

"I think we're past the word 'try,'" Sean admitted quietly. "How'd you know?"

"She's too tall. Male dwarves are really touchy about height. If you're a really tall one, you look for the shortest woman who'll have you."

"Why's that?"

"Tunnels. Notice how the hallways we walked down were only a few inches above your head?"

"Yeah, but the rooms here are huge."

"That's a sign of wealth," Roxy told him between bites; "to have space you don't need and can't use. But for the hallways and everything else? Most are lower than the ones we came here through. That's probably because they get more human visitors here and don't want them to feel claustrophobic."

Sean laughed, "I actually kind of like the feeling of being underground."

"That's your lycan side. We cats like dens, and dwarven communities are just like one big one to us."

"What about you?" Sean asked, nudging Jolene.

"For a tantric magic user, being underground is to be surround by the life of the earth," Jolene smiled at him, "So, yeah, I kind of like it too."

"First time, Jo?" Roxy asked.

Jolene nodded.

"Obviously not for you though, right?" Jolene asked Roxy, smiling.

"Nope, they're several large communities around Vegas; it's also where all the tin knockers come from."

"Tin knockers?" Sean asked, as Jolene looked on curious.

"They're the guys who do all the HVAC work in the high rises," Roxy told them. "You have to be small enough to fit into a lot of tight spaces, but strong enough to do some pretty heavy work. Dwarves are naturals at it, especially with their love of working metal."

"Huh, learn something new everyday," Sean said and added a "Thank you!" to Sarah as she dumped another pile of bacon, eggs, biscuits and gravy onto his plate.

Daelyn almost ran back to her room, she had a chain that would do Sean's gift justice, and she couldn't wait to put it on and see how it looked.

He'd given her a gift! She laughed and wondered if he knew the significance? The way he smiled, she had a sneaking suspicion that he knew exactly what he was up to. It was one thing to give a woman you were interested in a gift of jewelry, but to give her a magically enchanted one? Especially with such a powerful spell?

Oh, but there were going to be a lot of jealous women in the tunnels tonight! Daelyn couldn't help but laugh at that thought. Her uncle had been right, though. The way Sean's eyes locked on her, Daelyn smiled and sighed happily as she stepped into her home. No dwarven man had *ever* looked at her like that!

Going to her room she found the necklace she'd been thinking of, it was a one-inch band of delustered gold alloy, that would lay flat around the base of her neck, and dip down slightly over her chest, so the coin, once attached would hang right above her bosom. Clearly visible with the dress she was wearing.

Finding the proper attachment ring, it took her only a moment to wed the two pieces together, and then she quickly put it on and looked at it in the mirror.

The chain looked wonderful, the workmanship put into it was obvious, but the lack of shine on it drew one's eyes to the gold pendant attached there, the lion's head prominent.

Smiling, she turned back to the door, and then stopped for a moment. Going over to her closet she kicked off her low-heeled shoes and got out the pair of spike heels that she'd bought on a lark. Most dwarven women wore heels, because they were so short, but Daelyn always avoided them, because it made it clear to everyone else just how tall she was. She'd bought this set when she'd decided to go out to one of the casino bars and see what it was like, not being looked down on for her size. She still used them on occasion, but only when pressed into tour guide duty at the museum, something they often asked her to do because of her height she was sure.

Heading back to her uncles, for the first time in her life Daelyn strutted down the hall. Sure, in heels she was almost five-one, but for the first time in her life, that was going to be an advantage.

When Daelyn came back to the room, Sean sat up and once again stared.

"Whoa, she's hot," Jolene said, next to him.

"I'll say," Roxy agreed and then nudged Sean and smiled; teasing him, "go get her, Hon! Time to let the lion out!"

"Oh hell no, he can wait, I saw her first," Sean growled softly and getting up he walked over towards Daelyn and noticed she was now a bit taller than before. Letting his eyes look down those shapely legs he saw the rather sexy three-inch spike heels she was wearing, and looking back up at her, he smiled as she turned to look at him. The very fact that she'd put on something to accent her height, the one thing others held against her, made it clear to him that she had put them on just for him.

The other girls there were all looking at the medallion he'd given her, and seemed to be quite impressed. Sean would think that a gold medallion, even one that was made from a one-ounce coin wouldn't be that impressive to dwarves who worked precious metals regularly. Of course the chain she had it on was rather nice as well. So maybe it was the combination?

Walking up to Daelyn, he took her hands in his, and then bending over slightly he kissed her full on the lips in front of the others. He could feel his lion's approval.

"I like what you did with my gift," Sean said, smiling down at her as the others looked on.

"Well, I wanted to be sure it was on a strong chain, I wouldn't want to be without its enchantments," Daelyn replied with a wink.

"It's enchanted?" One of the girls who had been admiring the coin asked, sounding a bit surprised.

Sean turned and smiled, "Of course, made it myself. It protects one from being scryed on, as well as from spells that would attack the mind. Like say a sleep spell."

Sean was a little surprised that the eyes of *all* of the girls there widened, well Sarah's didn't, she just smiled a little wider and looked rather happy.

"Why don't you come sit with me," Sean said, returning his attention to Daelyn.

"I'd be delighted, Sean," Daelyn said and taking his arm he led her back to where he'd been sitting with Jolene and Roxy.

"Did I just make them all jealous?" Sean whispered to Daelyn as Roxy slid over so they could sit.

Daelyn giggled, a rather surprising sound. Sean found he kind of liked it.

"Most definitely. In human terms you just put a twenty carat perfect cut flawless blue-white diamond on my finger."

"Good," Sean smiled and helped her sit and then sat next to her, "Does this mean we're engaged?"

"Ummm," Daelyn suddenly blushed and both Jolene and Roxy snickered.

"What are *you* worried about?" Sean teased, "*I'm* trying to marry the gal who hit me in the face with a hammer. A *silver* hammer, mind you!"

"Just behave yourself, and you won't get hit again," Daelyn warned in a low voice.

"Oh, he behaves himself very well," Roxy whispered.

"In bed," Jolene added with a wink.

Sean put an arm around Daelyn, and hugged her, which stopped her from saying anything and just then the men showed up with the beer. Which was when the party really got started. Sean glanced at his watch; it was just past eleven, which mean he had definitely slept in a bit longer than normal. And while it may have seemed a bit early to start drinking to him, apparently it wasn't to anyone else. It wasn't long before he had a mug of beer in his hand and everyone was toasting to his good health.

As parties went, it was wonderful. Sean had never had a much in the way of birthday parties before, because he and his mom just couldn't afford it. She'd bake him a dozen cup cakes and put icing on them, and that was about the height of it. Not that Sean had minded, he appreciated it more that his mother had always taken his birthday off, and that they'd been able to spend the time together.

But today, today was wonderful. The beer in his mug was wonderful, and it was refilled as soon as he emptied it. Different foods and snacks were brought out all throughout the day, there was talking, there was music, there was even dancing, and Sean made damn sure to dance with all three of his women.

Of course he had to smile when that thought went through his head, he'd already decided that Daelyn was his, and after one rather slow dance with her he'd maneuvered her back into one of the darker corners and wrapping his arms around her, he'd kissed her long and hard.

She'd resisted a little, but not for long, and was returning it with interest by the time they both came up for air.

"Earth and stone, I hope nobody saw that," Daelyn sighed and leaned into him, "but damned if that wasn't worth the embarrassment."

"Daelyn," Sean whispered in her ear.

"Hmmm?"

"They all saw it, and if they didn't I'll happily drag you out into the center of the room so they can," Sean purred.

"You wouldn't!" Daelyn's whisper went higher in pitch.

"And anyone who makes fun of you for it, will be pounded into a nice bloody smear on the floor," Sean mock growled.

Daelyn sighed and leaned into him again, "I could get used to this."

"That *is* the general idea," Sean said and gave her a kiss on the forehead. He then danced another round with Jolene, who was a little unsteady on her feet from all the beer, and then Roxy who wasn't.

"Is Jo okay?" He asked Roxy.

"Eh, the alcohol is getting to her. She can't burn it off with magic the way we lycans do naturally. That's why she's not drinking as much as the rest of us."

Sean nodded, "Keep an eye on her; I'm a little preoccupied with Dae right now."

Roxy snickered, "Everyone is waiting for you to move in for the kill."

"What's that supposed to mean?"

"She's a virgin, and they all know you want her, and that she wants you. I think they're all a little surprised you haven't had your way with her yet. Especially now that everyone's heard about that little gift you gave her."

Sean smiled and gave Roxy a kiss, "Thanks for the heads up, I'll make sure I go easy on her the first time. As for moving 'in for the kill', she's mine, what's the rush? Right?"

Roxy laughed, "Taking pointers from your lion I see?"

"I'm learning," Sean agreed.

It wasn't much longer after that, that desserts were brought out, and apparently a present for him as well.

Sarah had just handed Sean a plate with a piece of cake on it that he was eating when Samis came over to him with a small package.

"What's that?" Sean asked, looking up from his seat.

"Your father gave this to me, a few months before he passed. He told me he wanted me to give this to you on your twenty-first birthday, or afterwards, if that wasn't possible."

"What is it?" Sean asked setting the plate down and taking the small velvet coated box. It had a thin metal band wrapped around the sides, and that was it.

"I have no idea. He told me that only you could open it."

Setting the box down, Sean stood up and gave Samis a hug.

"Thank you, Samis. Thank you very much for giving that to me."

"You're welcome, Sean. Your father, he was a good man, but unfortunately he was too trusting, and in some ways, too naive perhaps. He didn't realize the trouble he'd gotten both himself and his family in, until it was too late. So he did what he could to try and protect you, and pass on his legacy.

"When he gave me that, he told me to tell you that there is a world of difference between justice and vengeance. That when you burn the world down, you burn your own home with it. But," Samis smiled then, "if you ever do find yourself with the power to exact justice, he won't complain if you get a little revenge on those that wronged your family as well."

"Thanks, Samis. Yes, there's definitely going to be a little vengeance before I get through with all of this, I'm sure."

"I remember you as a child, Sean. You're almost a member of the family."

Sean smiled and turned to look at Daelyn, as she sat eating a piece of cake and talking with Roxy and Jolene.

"Just how sound proof are the rooms here?"

"It's solid rock, Sean, so very."

Sean nodded slowly, "I think it's time to unwrap my other birthday present."

Samis laughed again, "Have a good night!"

"Oh, I plan on it," Sean grinned and picking up the box and putting it in his pocket he walked over to the girls.

"What was in the box?" Jolene asked.

"Something from my dad," Sean told them, "Samis has been holding on to it for I guess thirteen years now."

"Aren't you going to open it?" Daelyn asked, looking up at him.

"There are some things more important, Love. It can wait until morning," reaching down Sean took Daelyn's plate as she stared at him with wide eyes and handed it to Roxy, then carefully pulling her up out of her seat he kissed her long and hard in front of everyone.

"Time for bed, my love," he whispered in her ear, then sweeping her up in to a bridal carry, Sean took her back to the room they'd been staying in.

"Don't I get a say in this?" Daelyn asked, still looking up in shocked surprise.

"Daelyn?"

"Yes?"

"Don't be a brat."

"Yes, Dear," Daelyn smiled a little nervously as Sean entered the room and kicked the door closed behind him.

"You're my first," she admitted shyly to him.

"I'll be gentle," Sean promised and setting her back on her feet he started to kiss her again, only this time he let his fingers take the tab on the zipper on the back of her dress and slowly pull it down, until it stopped just above that lovely ass of hers.

Pulling the top of the dress off of her shoulders, Sean took a step back and watched as the dress just pooled around her feet. Surprisingly, she wasn't wearing anything at all beneath it, and the sight of her standing there, wearing nothing more than her heels made the breath catch in his throat. Sean wondered once again just what in the world he had done to deserve such beautiful women in his life.

Pulling his shirt off and then pushing his own pants down as he kicked off his shoes, Sean leaned down and kissed her lightly, then he gently put his hands on her body and started to slowly stroke her, cupping those magnificent breasts as he moved closer, slowly closing the space between them, until he wrapped his arms around her, reaching down to give that lovely butt of hers a squeeze.

Picking her up again, he carried Daelyn over to the bed, and carefully laid her down on it. Smiling at her, he carefully got on the bed again, and kissed her once more, while allowing his hands to explore the smooth flesh of her body, only this time he let his mouth join the exploration. He was in no rush, and it wasn't long before Daelyn started to run her hands through his hair as he moved down her body, taking the time to worship every last inch of it.

Using the tricks that Jolene and Roxy had both taught him, he had Daelyn sighing contentedly before he even started in on her sex with his mouth, which turned those sighs into loud moans.

Eventually when she urged him up, he covered her body with his and slowly eased his hardness into her, being careful and starting off slow. He discovered that yes, Daelyn was a virgin. He also soon discovered that she wanted him as much as he wanted her and all shyness evaporated as she loudly goaded him on, encouraging him rather enthusiastically as they both got rather physical and Sean was reminded once again just how strong his little Daelyn was and when they both finally reached their peak together, he collapsed on top of her panting and kissing her as she panted and kissed him back.

"So, is that what all the fuss is about?" Daelyn said with a sweaty grin. "Hardly seems worth the trouble."

"Oh, in that case, I guess I'll just go back to the party," Sean said while faking a yawn.

"I've heard it gets better with practice? Maybe we should try again?" Daelyn giggled.

Sean made it look like he was pondering the idea, "Well, I guess another ten or twenty times wouldn't hurt."

Daelyn blinked and looked at him, "Ten? or *Twenty?*"

Sean smirked, "The extra wives aren't for my benefit, they're for yours. Us lions, we just can't help ourselves you know, now come here, Love! If you're still able to talk, obviously I'm not doing something right!"

Several hours had passed and Daelyn was lying on the bed, panting in a pool of sweat and other things, with Sean wrapped around her, when Roxy and Jolene finally came into the room.

"Any regrets?" Roxy chuckled as she started to undress.

"Not a one," Sean purred.

"I wasn't talking to you!" Roxy laughed and threw her top at him.

"Can I keep him?" Daelyn gasped and shivered, "I think I found something better than driving my 'Cuda."

"Just as long as you promise to share," Jolene said as she and Roxy joined them on the bed.

"Ummm..." Daelyn said and looked at the other two.

"Relax," Sean said and kissed her, "nothing will happen unless you want it to."

"You happened."

"Well, yeah. But you wanted it to!"

It was late, Sean had come back from the bathroom and instead of pulling the case out of his pocket, he pulled out his cell phone. He was surprised to see that it was still in one piece.

Looking at it he debated putting the battery in it and checking his messages. It had been a week and he really did need to go see Chad and talk some strategy, probably get John to fix his phone so no one could track him, and he definitely needed to tell Steve to pick up the Mercedes.

But this far underground, he was sure there wouldn't be a signal, so with a sigh, he stuck it back in his pocket and pulled out the case his father had left for him. There was a small metal bump on the side, and when he touched it with his finger, a small spark jumped out of the bump and ran all around the side of the box, right in the middle of the metal strip encircling it.

When it came back to where it had started, the box split in two and a ring lay in the bottom half. Picking it up, Sean examined it. It wasn't gold, and it wasn't silver. Best he could guess was tungsten perhaps? Putting it on, he was surprised when it instantly resized to fit his finger. Calling up his monitor program, he could see that like the watch, it wasn't trying to do anything to him.

Concentrating on it, like the watch, didn't do anything either, so laying down next to Daelyn he curled up between her and Roxy, and went back to sleep.

"Hello, Son."

Sean opened his eyes, he was back in the classroom, and his father was there once more.

"You've obviously been given the ring I left with Samis, and put it on. I actually made several of these, but I wasn't sure which one you'd end up with. The seer that I hired to try and discern the future, your future, told me there were just too many variables.

"That's why I didn't leave my notes with Samis, or with anyone else. I just didn't feel safe with that many copies lying around. You see, Son, I found the answer! Actually I found several answers, to questions I hadn't even been looking for! And I uncovered a few secrets that are the kind of thing that a father only passes down to his son. The kind of thing best not shared widely, or there will be those who misuse it to terrible ends.

"So yes, I found a way to protect lycans from silver; it was childishly simple, and also terribly difficult. And along the way I discovered how to unlock power, some real power, and possibly terrible power. Again it was so obvious and so simple, but also incredibly dangerous to do just right. Something that had been right before all of our eyes for over sixty years, but no one made the connection.

"No one but your old man, apparently.

"Unfortunately, making each of the devices I wanted to give to my lycan friends takes time, way too much time. I made one, to prove the concept, but it took me a year! The second one only took nine months, but there was no way I could find to make it any faster, and obviously my time ran out before I discovered the answer.

"My second device, my notes, they're all sealed in a box, under a cement flower urn. You'll have to unscrew it, better bring a friend, I had Sampson help me with it, damn thing was far too heavy for me! He won't remember it, so don't ask him about it, I wiped the whole affair from his mind, with his consent of course.

"So to get it out, turn it clockwise a quarter turn while pushing down on it. Then pull it up and turn counter-clockwise the same amount, then simply lift it up.

"As for the location, what's the last view that they'll ever see? Go to the center of that, and you'll find the urn. Sorry for the riddle, Son, but for all that I've keyed this just to you, I still worry about the wrong person finding this.

"I have one last caution, one warning: I want to set the lycans free, but I do not want them to war upon the wizards and the mages and my fellow users of magic. I know some are going to seek reprisals, and perhaps some of those reprisals will be justified.

"But don't let it turn into a war.

"Good luck, Son. I love you; I hope this finds you well."

Saturday, in the Park

Sean was woken up rather early by Daelyn, who having just lost her virginity was apparently interested in making up for lost time.

Of course neither Roxy nor Jolene wanted to be left out, though Daelyn wasn't exactly comfortable with sharing him at the same time, so they were all careful enough not to push that.

But it didn't mean Daelyn didn't watch when he was busy with the other two.

"Doesn't he ever run down?" Daelyn asked Roxy when he was finally allowed to head off to the bathroom.

"Oh, eventually," Roxy teased. "That's why he eats so much all the time!"

Sean just sighed and hit the shower, then went and had breakfast while the girls each got cleaned up.

"So, what are your plans?" Samis asked, after Sean had finished eating and the girls had come out to join them.

"Well, I need to go find this legacy of mine," Sean told them, "but I also need to find a safe place for us to stay."

"We can live in my home," Daelyn said.

Sean shook his head as Samis frowned. "Maybe one day," Sean said, "but not right now. What I'm doing has the potential to get ugly, and I don't think the leaders of your community would appreciate being drug into it by my living here."

Daelyn looked at her uncle who nodded in agreement.

"Sean is right. This is not a problem for us dwarves. Not yet at least. Eventually our leaders may wish to take a stand, but I've already consulted with them, and for now, they wish to remain neutral. You can visit, but you can't live here."

"Well, that sucks!" Daelyn grumbled.

Sean put his hand on her leg, "It's okay, Hon. This is our problem, not theirs. It wouldn't be fair to drag them into the middle of it."

Daelyn sighed, and then blushed as she looked at her uncle and her aunt who were both smiling. Pulling her leg away, she glared at Sean, or tried to.

"You get used to it," Jolene whispered into her ear, leaning over.

"Get used to what?" Daelyn growled softly back.

"Being his, of course. Don't worry, took me a week to admit it."

Daelyn looked at Sean who smiled at her warmly.

"We only slept together once!"

"Actually, it was more like ten times," Sean corrected.

"You know what I mean!" Daelyn blushed as her aunt and uncle laughed.

"So," Roxy interrupted, turning to Samis, "any suggestions on where we should go?"

"Actually, yes, I have one," Samis began, drawing everyone's attention. "Back in the fifties, there was a lot of concern about nuclear war and such. So there was a lot of scrambling to build fallout shelters."

"Ugh, I've been in a few of those, they're pretty rundown now," Sean said.

Samis nodded, "Yes, most of them are. But not the ones the dwarves built.

"What in the world did we need fallout shelters for?" Daelyn asked.

"Oh, they weren't for us, they were for those who were friends of the dwarves and were willing to pay us to ease their concerns." Samis shrugged, "It was a different time then, I was just a young boy."

"And it's still there?" Sean asked.

Samis nodded, "The entrance is concealed using an old drainage tunnel that goes under South Virginia Street; along one of the old stretches just sound of town. There used to be a house to the west of it, but that was torn down ages ago."

"Well, wouldn't hurt to check it out," Sean said looking at the girls who all nodded. "Where is it? And how do we get in?"

Samis got out a map then and told them how to find it, as well as how to open it.

"Well, might as well get started," Sean said, after that. "Thank you, Samis, for everything, I really do appreciate it."

"Anytime, Sean, you're a member of the family now," he said with a wink and looked over at his niece, Daelyn who blushed, "as well as a friend."

"Any idea what might convince those in charge to take our side?" Roxy asked while standing up and stretching.

"Two things," Samis said, "the first is to show them that you really can do what your father set out to do."

"And the other?"

"Doing it. The biggest fear of the casters is that this will lead to a war, a war against them, because many of them have much to feel guilty over. If you start this, and ask for our help, I'm sure that they will give it, but only to prevent that war from taking place.

"The world is too small, too crowded, for a conflict like that to go unnoticed. It would endanger many of us as it spread."

Sean nodded, "I'll be sure to keep that in mind."

"May the living powers of the Earth guide you, and the strength of the Stone protect you, Sean."

Sean smiled, "Thank you," then looked around at the others, "let's go."

"Well, it's not much to look at," Jolene shrugged shining a light spell around, "but at least it's dry."

Sean nodded and looked around the main room. The place was actually rather large, there was a hidden underground garage that Daelyn had been able to drive her car into, with enough space to park a couple more. Then there had been a stairway behind a heavy door that led down to the main room, which had a hallway with several 'suites' off of it, as well as a large kitchen area.

"So, all it needs is power and water," Sean said looking around.

"It's got those," Daelyn said pointing over to a large green panel set in the wall by the main door. "Just open that and open the valves."

Sean looked at her, "What? Seriously?"

Daelyn laughed, "What, you think they wouldn't build this place just like we build our own communities? Where do you think we get our water and power from?"

Sean shrugged, "I have no idea, honestly."

Daelyn went over to the panel and opened it. Inside there were two large valves, she started opening them both.

"One of these is for water, the one with the green handle. The blue one, that's for power. There's lots of geothermal in the area, and this opens the feed to generate steam for the turbine generator."

"How long will it take?" Roxy said, shining her flashlight around.

Daelyn shrugged, "Depends on how much work they put into it. I'd guess anywhere between a half-hour to two hours."

"Well, let's take a look around and see what we're going to need," Sean said, shining his flashlight around. The furniture, if you could call it that, was mostly made out of stone and set along the walls.

"Gonna need a lot of cushions," Jolene sighed.

"And some air mattresses!" Roxy called out from one of the 'suites' she was shining her light into. "The beds are all made out of stone as well."

"With no one down here to care for it, wood furniture would have rotted," Daelyn said. "The bed you slept on last night was made from stone; it just had a good mattress on it."

"What's this door at the back for?" Roxy asked, shining a light over a door that looked more like a dogged hatchway.

"That probably leads down to the equipment room, wells, turbine, a small shop, and the emergency exit," Daelyn said coming over and undogging the hatch she opened it and shined her flashlight down a circular staircase.

"Yup. I'll go down and check it out once we have power."

"Emergency exit?" Sean asked.

Daelyn nodded, "Always gotta have a backdoor. In case the front one is blocked."

"Well that's good to know!"

"So, while we're waiting for power," Roxy said and came back over to Sean, "How about you tell us what you learned from your ring?"

Sean nodded and went over to sit on one of the stone 'seats' cut into the wall.

"First of all, whatever it was that my father was trying to make, he succeeded."

"Really?" Roxy's eyes got wide. "What does it do?"

Sean shrugged, "I don't know, he didn't say. He told me he made two, the first one took him a year, the second one nine months, and that the second one was with his notes."

"Nine months?" Jolene shook her head, "That'll never be practical, not when you'll need to make thousands of the thing."

"What about that archival spell of his, Jo? Wouldn't that let him make them faster?"

Jolene nodded, "Good point," she turned back to Sean, "Did he say what he did with the first one?"

Sean shook his head, "No, he didn't."

"So where is it?" Daelyn asked.

Sean shrugged again, "I have no idea. He was too paranoid of someone else getting their hands on the ring, that he only left me a couple of clues. The problem is, I have no idea what the first one means."

"Well what is it?" Roxy asked.

"He said that 'as for the location, it's the last view that they'll ever see,' whatever that means."

"The last view that *who* will ever see?" Roxy asked.

Sean shrugged again.

"Ugh, I hate riddles," Daelyn sighed.

"Well, I have an idea," Jolene said.

"Really? What?"

"How about we go out and get something soft to sit on, before all of our asses become flat!" Jolene grumbled.

Sean laughed, "That would be a true crime against humanity *and* the world."

"Exactly!"

"Umm, you know my car doesn't have a very large trunk," Daelyn warned.

"We can hit a camping goods store," Roxy told them. "A few rolled up foam mattresses, some sleeping bags, some pillows; we'll be fine for now."

"Yeah, I guess we can fit that," Daelyn agreed, "and by the time we get back, the power should be on. If not," Daelyn shrugged, "I'm sure I can fix it."

They went out, closing the doors behind them, and getting into Daelyn's car they headed off to do a little shopping.

"Where's a payphone, when you need one?" Sean sighed looking around as they shopped.

"What do you need a payphone for?" Daelyn asked.

"I want to call a friend, and I'm afraid if I use my cell phone, they'll track it to him."

"Ah, then you need one of these," Daelyn said and steered him down an aisle where they had pre-paid cell phones."

"Oh! Right, been meaning to get one of those."

"Grab a bunch," Daelyn said and flagged over a salesperson.

Twenty minutes later, Sean was dialing Steve's work number.

"Bryson's, Steve speaking."

"Hey, Steve. I had to abandon the Mercedes, late Thursday night in Carson City."

"Oh, yeah, I know," Steve sighed, "I got a phone call from the motel, they said they found it sitting in their parking lot this morning. They were worried about it being stolen, as the people who showed up in it, left it there. You had me worried there, Sean."

"Yeah, apparently someone's got a trace on my debit card and they followed us there. I would have let you know sooner, but well, I've been busy."

"I told Chad about your problem, by the way."

Sean sighed, "He thinks you're crazy now, doesn't he?"

Steve laughed, "Oh, does he ever! I got a big bet going with him now! You know that Nintendo world championship cartridge of his?"

"Steve, you didn't!"

"Of course I did. Put my old twenty-six hundred console up against it! You'd think he'd know better than to bet against me!"

Sean just shook his head and sighed, "So, what'd he say?"

"Well, he said that if I wasn't crazy, that he had a few ideas, I think he mentioned helots, or something like that."

"I'll call him or something. One last question?"

"Sure, shoot."

"Gotta riddle: What's the last view they'll ever see? Does that mean anything to you?"

"Beats me, ask Chad, he's better at that kind of thing than I am!"

"Okay, bye," Sean hung up the phone.

"So, learn anything?" Roxy asked.

Sean shook his head, "Not really, no."

By the time they got back to their new hideout, the power had come on, and there was light as well as hot water. Sean left the girls to take care of things as he found a place to get comfortable and then went into his classroom. There was so much he had to learn, so much that he needed to know, but the problem was, he had no idea what to study next.

He checked his stats first, but it'd only been a few days since he'd last checked them, so of course there'd been no changes there. After that he looked at the books that had been left to him, there were thirty-nine of them, if he counted the beginner's primer, and while he understood enough to learn any of them, the problem was that he didn't have the time right now to learn all of them.

So which was he to pick?

Or should he just forgo them all, and make up his spells on the spot? The problem with that was that it took longer to cast those spells, and used more energy. The limiting factor for mages everywhere Sean had learned was energy. This was why they used the spells in the books, which were easier to learn, and which had been designed to conserve as much energy as possible.

It also explained why they used weapons or magical items against him in most of his conflicts with them, more than they had magic. Jolene's uncle was probably the only one who'd gone straight to magic, but then, his actions had been more for the purposes of showing off than for winning any kind of fight.

Now, as a magic using lycan, Sean was their worst nightmare, because lycans had lots of magical energy, which was what allowed them to change. And it was that very nature that tended to keep magic users from becoming lycans, as their magical ability normally seized hold of the 'infection' and drained it dry of magic, thus killing it, before it could transform the magic user into one.

And the magic users most certainly did *not* allow lycans to learn magic, lest they be overwhelmed. Sean also suspected that there might be other reasons as well why lycans avoided magic. What those were however, he had no idea.

He ended up deciding to learn as many of the different healing spells that there were for now. Daelyn couldn't regenerate, and if Jolene ever got injured, he'd have to do something for her as well. Plus it taught him the magic of the living flesh, as well as how to manipulate it, and surely that would be useful at some point.

He felt someone shaking him eventually, and when he opened his eyes, Jolene was smiling down at him. She was naked.

"Mmm?" Sean said looking her over.

"I have an idea on just how to solve that little riddle of yours," Jolene smiled back and started to undo his pants.

"Sure you do," Sean chuckled.

"What, don't want me to try?" she paused, smirking up at him.

"Now I didn't say that, did I?"

Jolene laughed, "No, no you didn't."

Crawling onto the foam mattress they'd put down over one of the stone beds, Jolene slowly kissed her way up his body, until eventually she reached his lips and Sean put his arms around her and kissed her back lovingly.

They took their time, and as Sean felt the power start to build, Jolene took him on a slow journey through his memories, searching for that one phrase, or something like it.

Sean found it very fascinating, apparently some parts of his mind remembered things so much better than he ever had.

"Blame the geas for that," Jolene whispered in his ear.

All Sean could do was kiss her back, thanking her for restoring to him more of what his father had been, and what his father had meant to him. The geas and the years had turned Sean's father into a perfect stranger, and now, finally, he was able to remember the man who had once been so important to him.

Sean relived much of his childhood then, his childhood from before the death of his father, after which he'd had to start working in order to help his mother pay the bills and put food on the table.

His father had been a larger than life figure, and not just because Sean had been a small boy. With the experience that he now had, he could tell that many of his father's friends had been non-humans. The people they would go off to meet, or who would come over for dinner or for parties, there were dwarves, lycans, some tall fair race that Sean hadn't yet met (*'Elves,'* Jolene supplied), and other magic users.

There were also famous people, politicians, interesting and eccentric folks, and then beings that Sean couldn't remember clearly and for which Jolene couldn't help him.

In all of this, Sean could see that his father was held in high regard by so many of these people, though none as great as the lycans. That he was warm and generous with everyone, and that he never raised his voice, never used a mean or even harsh word, with anyone, and was always fast to forgive.

It was no wonder that they had hired a man from far away to kill him, Sean realized. Any local, even if they'd had the power, would never have been able to go through with it, his father was too charismatic, too friendly, it would have been like killing a member of your own family.

Sean again had to laugh at the pure folly of those who had put the geas on him, blocking away so many of the things his father had taught him. If

Sean had been able to retain those lessons during his formative years, he doubted that he'd be thinking many of the thoughts he was today.

He hadn't lied when he'd agreed with Samis that a war was a bad idea.

But he still planned on waging one against every person who had been involved in his father's murder. The lessons Sean had learned after many years of struggling and suffering had been very clear, and the biggest was that you paid back those who wronged you, whenever you could, and as Roxy and his lion had taught him, you never suffered an enemy to live.

They were up to the last of the memories in Sean's mind, one of Sean and his father off in a rather green place, in the early spring. A place that Sean had only been to twice before.

"Dad, why do they call this place Mountain View?" Sean asked his father as they visited the gravesite of his grandfather and grandmother.

"Because it has such a wonderful view of them," his father had replied.

"Why would they want to have a view of the mountains?"

"Well, what would you want your last view to be? The one that you'll watch for eternity? Things come and go, but mountains endure."

Sean opened his eyes and grabbed Jolene's hips.

"I know where we need to go now!" He said, excitedly.

Jolene wrapped her legs around him tightly then. "You're not going anywhere until you finish here first!" She laughed.

Sean smiled and kissed her, "Oh don't worry, I need to be sure and *thank* you now, rather thoroughly, don't I?"

Saturday Night

"You know, we really need to get a bigger car," Roxy spoke up from the back seat as they heading into Sparks.

"I'm not giving up my 'Cuda!" Daelyn grumbled.

"Who said anything about giving it up?" Roxy replied. "We just need another, and larger, car. We need to go food shopping and see about stocking our home."

"And clothes shopping!" Jolene piped up "I'm out of outfits! Again!"

Sean rolled his eyes as he listened to the girls go back and forth in the car. They were on their way to Chad's place. It was Saturday, gaming night, and while Sean wasn't crazy about the idea of exposing all of his gaming friends to the new realities of his life, the fact was he needed Chad's help, and it was too late to go raiding graveyards with the sun down. That would draw the police like flies. Better off to wait until tomorrow, during the daylight.

"We need another car," Sean sighed, drawing an immediately end to that part of the debate. Sean was still getting used to the weight that his words seemed to be gaining with the girls as the days went by.

"You'll let me pick it out, right?" Daelyn told him.

Sean nodded, "Anyone who can maintain a car like this definitely knows more about cars than I do."

Daelyn smiled, "Thanks!"

Sean listened with half an ear as the girls then debated what *kind* of car to get. The only thing that Daelyn was willing to agree on was making it an automatic, which made Sean happy, as he'd never learned how to drive a stick. He hadn't even gotten his license until he'd gone to college and suspected he was probably the worst driver of the four of them. Well, maybe not Jolene, he still didn't know if she owned a car or not.

When they pulled up in front of Chad's house, Daelyn carefully backed into the driveway. Sean noticed Alex's and John's cars parked in the street in front of the house. Chad's girlfriend's car wasn't there, but then she rarely came over on game night.

"Well, time to face the music," Sean sighed.

"Why are *you* so nervous?" Daelyn asked.

"Because I'm about to walk in there, and show my very human friends that not only do I now have *three* wives, but that I'm not even human anymore."

"Three?" Daelyn asked with a grumble, looking at him.

Sean turned to her and smiling he leaned over the center console and taking her head in his hands he kissed her, as he slowly counted to thirty.

When he released her, Daelyn blinked and looked a little disorientated as Roxy and Jolene laughed.

"Three," Sean smiled and patted her on the leg, then opening the door he got out and tipped the seat forward and helped Jolene get out. Gathering them up, he walked up to the front door of the house, knocked once, and then went inside.

It was after nine, so they were deep into the campaign when Sean walked into the room. Chad was the first to look up from the table, as the front door was in his direct line of sight.

"Sean!" He called out as Sean entered, "Where you been hiding? We heard you gotta new girlfriend!"

Sean noticed that only Alex and John were there, Zack either hadn't made it tonight, or had left earlier.

Chad got up and came around the table as both Alex and John looked up. Roxy was dressed pretty normally for her, a t-shirt that didn't hide any of her charms, a pair of shorts that showed off her legs and her butt, and a pair of sneakers. Jolene, well Jolene was wearing skintight jeans with another of those low cut and loose fitting blouses that Sean had noticed she seemed to like, with a pair of sneakers as well.

As for Daelyn, she was actually wearing a dress with heels. Mainly because Sean had vetoed her going out in her coveralls. She looked rather stunning in it, even with her hair done up in a thick braid that reached down to her ass. Of course she was wearing the same thing under the dress that she wore under the coveralls, namely, nothing.

Chad smiled at Sean and gave him a hug, "I'd ask which one of these lovely women is your girlfriend, but I have a sinking feeling that I just lost a rather large bet!"

Sean smiled and shook his head, even when he lost, Chad didn't bitch. He was always happy, and almost always there with a smile.

"Girlfriends?" John said from the table as he got up, "as in plural?"

"Yowza!" Alex laughed, also standing, "and I was already jealous when I heard about him and Roxy!"

Sean nodded, "Girlfriends, or to put it more aptly," Sean smiled at Daelyn, who blushed, "wives. This is Roxy, former trackstar and werecheetah. Next is Jolene, who is a tantric witch, and rather accomplished if I say so myself," Sean grinned as Jolene winked at the guys. "And last, but definitely not least, is Daelyn. She's a dwarf, if perhaps a little tall for a female, but she definitely lets me hold it against her every night," Sean smiled at Daelyn who blushed and then swatted him on the ass.

"Wow!," Alex said, "Female gamers!"

"Umm," Chad said and looked each of the girls over and then looked at Sean, "I'm a little surprised that you came by tonight. I thought you'd want to have kept it a little more secret."

Sean shrugged, "I've known all of you since junior high, you're my friends, if I can't trust you, well, who can I? Besides, no one's going to believe you anyway, right?"

"Wait," Alex said, "what's he talking about?"

John sighed, "He didn't tell us what characters they played, he told us what they are."

"Huh?" Alex said looking around the room at everybody.

Sean looked at John, surprised. "You know?"

"Course I know," John nodded, "I know you guys all think I'm a conspiracy nut, but half my customers are either lycans or dwarves. Hell, I even get the occasional elf."

"How'd that happen?" Chad asked looked at John, a bit surprised himself.

"Eh, you know I do a lot of security systems work with my dad, well I started doing a bunch of side work under the table for a goblin," John shrugged and grinned, "the money was good and the work was challenging as hell. Didn't really care that he wasn't human, besides, I grew up on stories about all that kind of stuff, my parents are Indians after all. Apparently I have a great grandfather who was an elf or something."

"Sawyer, right?" Sean asked, looking at John.

"Yup, that's the one. Guy's a laugh, always telling people how much he hates humans, when he really just hates magic users."

"Whoa, whoa, wait a moment," Alex said looking at John, "Roxy is a werecheetah?"

"Yup," Sean said, "and since I got bit, I'm a werelion."

"Well, that explains the girlfriends," John said with a shrug.

"You know," Chad said, thinking a moment, "Steve did say you only had two wives, I wonder if I could void the bet now that you have three...."

"Hold on!" Alex said looking around, "I want some proof, before I start thinking you're all just putting one over on me!"

Sean shrugged and shifted, noticing that Roxy did the same.

"Impressive," Chad said looking up at Sean, "Watch out for the chandelier!"

"Holy..." Alex said, and looked at Sean first then at Roxy. Then he sat back down in his chair, rather hard. "This is gonna take some getting used to."

Sean shrugged and growled, "Hey, how do ya' think I feel? I *am* one now."

Alex snorted, "You're big, buff, and got three wives who are all hot as hell, excuse me if I fail to see your problem, Sean!"

"Right now," Chad said looking over at Alex, "there are a lot of people who want Sean dead. As they're all magic users, I'd say that's a hell of a problem, wouldn't you?"

Alex grumbled, "Okay, you got a point. Still," Alex looked over at Roxy, Jolene, and Daelyn, "with three women like that at your side, I somehow don't think you'll in all that much trouble."

"Yeah, we are pretty kick-ass," Roxy grinned.

Chad motioned for everyone to sit down at the table, "Well, I guess we're done with gaming for tonight. So, Sean, tell me about this problem Steve told me you're having."

"Sean," John spoke up, "while he's doing that, how about you let me take a look at your phone?"

Sean nodded and handed John his phone, and the battery.

"Ah! Smart man, pulled the battery. Let me get my stuff from the car and I'll fix it for you, while you and Chad talk strategy."

"What are you going to fix?" Daelyn asked, curious.

"Take out the GPS, disable the camera, the wifi, the microphone, make sure no one can snoop on him or trace him easily when he uses it."

"Oh, cool! Can I watch?"

"Hell's yeah. I'll even do your phone if you want."

Sean grinned and shook his head as the two of them went off talking tech.

"So," Sean started, "This is what I know," and he proceeded to tell Chad almost everything about the last two weeks.

After Sean had finished, Chad was looking thoughtful, while Alex looked rather surprised, and John was showing Daelyn some tricks with her phone, having already finished with Sean's, Roxy's, and Jolene's.

"First off, I'm sorry to hear about what happened to your father," Chad said. "Even after all of these years, I'm sure it must hurt to find out the truth."

Sean sighed and nodded at that as both Alex and John offered their sympathies as well.

"That said, how often do the magic users just out and out kill lycans? Is it common? Do they regularly go out there and reduce the numbers?"

Sean shrugged and looked at Roxy, "Rox? Do you know?"

"Well," Roxy said, "if you upset a magic user enough, and you're one of 'their' lycans, yeah, they'll kill you on the spot. If you belong to another mage," she shrugged, "it depends. If you're a free one, well that depends on if they think they have the power to kill you or not. But free lycans avoid magic users like the plague, because no one wants to end up serving one."

"So, just how do they keep the numbers down?" Chad asked her.

"They don't have to. There are so many different races of us, and we're so spread out, that it's not uncommon for a lot of us to never hook up with someone we can have children with, or to not even try hooking up. Raising a lycan family is tough, not a lot want to do it."

Alex spoke up then, "Why are there free lycans? Why aren't they all in thrall to a magic user?"

"Because there are just too many of us," Roxy said, "and a lot of us just won't stand for it. We outnumber them, they know it, and some of us are willing to launch an all out offensive against any coven or group that steals one of our family."

"Then why haven't you freed the others?"

"Any fight to free anyone is always going to be a bloody one, possibly with several deaths on both sides," Roxy said and shook her head, "who would want to risk their lives for anyone who isn't a member of your immediate family?"

"So," Chad said, "In short, you're too fractious to work together, as a whole, to stop the magic users from keeping some of you as slaves."

Roxy nodded, "That's about the height of it. Plus they don't tend to grab just any lycan; there are lycan families that have been under the dominance of certain families or counsels for centuries."

"And how to they enforce compliance?"

"Again, it varies," Roxy sighed. "Some are just out and out slaves, and if they act up, they'll be killed. It's a favorite trick of some groups to put a ceramic capsule into the body of their lycan slaves, that is magicked and easily broken open when needed to kill the lycan by introducing pure powdered silver into their blood.

"Others," Roxy shrugged, "they've either been conditioned from birth to follow orders, or perhaps have family members held hostage, or in some all too rare cases, they're there willingly, because they're treated well."

"So, it's not exactly like the Helots," Chad said.

"Steve mentioned that word," Sean said. "Who were they?"

"The Spartans had a subclass of people called Helots. They did all the farming and everything else that a military society that can't be bothered with, basically they handled the nuts and bolts of survival that the Spartans needed. But they out numbered the Spartans by quite a bit. As the Spartan's society continued, they began to fear the Helots, because of their greater numbers and good physical condition from working hard all day.

"So eventually they'd declare war on them, once a year or so, and during that time, any Spartan could strike down any Helot, without fear of moral reprimand or drawing the ire of their gods. More than once there was an organized culling of the ranks as well. It doesn't sound like the magic users have gotten to that point at least. But the striking down of anyone who angers them...."

"Or who they fear," Sean interjected, remembering the recent storm.

"Or who they fear," Chad nodded and continued, "has certainly led to a lot of hate against them, I'm sure. Which, regardless of if you're successful or not, is going to lead to a lot of recriminations, and deaths."

Sean shrugged, "As long as they kill the right people, I don't really care."

Sean noticed he got a couple of looks from the girls when he said that, though Roxy's was in obvious agreement. Jolene looked a little worried, and Daelyn looked a little sad.

"Okay," Chad nodded, "but, *who are the right ones?*"

"The ones who were involved in my father's murder, of course."

"Ah," Chad said, "but what about the ones involved in the murder of other lycans? Are they the right ones too?"

"Probably," Sean agreed.

"Well, then you're going to be in trouble," Chad warned him. "Because from the sounds of things, that's going to probably be the majority of the magic users out there."

"Oh, I doubt it's that many!" Sean said, shaking his head.

"If you don't do a thing to stop it, are you not involved? If you accept it? If you make jokes about it? If you don't speak out against it? You're dealing with a very slippery slope here, Sean. At some point, you're going to have to draw a line. If you can't get the majority of the magic users on your side, the odds of your winning are zero."

"But we out number them!"

Chad shrugged, "But they're in the entrenched position, they have the power, and I don't doubt government, on their side. The simple fact that the practice is still going on, shows that you're fighting an uphill battle."

Sean sighed, "Fine. But the ones directly involved in my father's death, they're not getting away."

"Chad," Jolene spoke up. "Just how many slave revolts have succeeded in history?

"Well," Chad sighed, "technically only one."

"Only one!"

"What do you mean 'technically,'" Sean asked.

"Well, Haiti was founded because the slaves there all revolted, and eventually gained independence. Then there was the Baptist War in Jamaica, which while they lost, Britain outlawed slavery the next year, so in effect you could claim that they won. Then there was the escaped slave Gaspar Yanga, he founded a colony that lasted forty years, during which he was an outlaw and fought with the Spanish, until he negotiated a peace treaty with the Spanish, who in return for him paying taxes, recognized his town."

"So the odds are against us then," Sean sighed.

"Hey, you've got me on your side!" Chad laughed, "And from the sound of it, the dwarves at least would like to see you succeed. You see, the problem comes when the reparations and retaliations start. If the majority of magic users think that they have no choice but to fight, they'll fight. But if they think that it's just more trouble than it's worth, they won't."

"I don't think they're going to want to give up their slaves," Jolene warned.

"Hey, it's the twenty-first century. People have been opposed to slavery for nearly two centuries in this country, same for most of the world. These people don't live in a vacuum, I'm sure a lot of their kids don't care for it, so they'll start facing pressure at home.

"And," Chad smiled, "if Sean here can in fact remove their hold over the lycans, well they'll be in a position of preferring to sue for peace over one of going to war. The key," Chad turned to face Sean, "is you will need to enforce that peace once it comes. And this isn't going to be easy for a very long time."

Sean sighed, if there was one thing he'd learned about Chad, it was that he was damn near always right about anything dealing with politics, war, or people. It was one of the things that made him such a gaming genius. Chad always outguessed and outmaneuvered those around him, more than once he'd told Sean in whispers exactly what his opponent was going to do in a gaming match.

And because Chad had his kneecap shattered in a senseless retaliation by a gang member who had mistaken Chad for somebody else back when he was in high school, he knew that Chad had serious issues with random and senseless violence. Chad had wanted to go into the military and prove that when it came to tactics, he was the best.

Now he was permanently four-F.

"Okay, fine. If I promise to do everything I can to stop there from being any recriminations, once things settle down, will you help me?"

Chad smiled, "Of course, you know I'll never get another chance to run a war."

Sean nodded, "I promise."

"Ah, good! Now, let's make some plans!"

Sean reached into his pocket and dug out three of the enchanted gold coins, he'd enchanted the rest of them earlier, just in case.

"Get a chain, and wear these from now on," he said and handed one to Chad, one to Alex, and one to John.

"What are they?"

"Protection from scrying, and mind spells. Like I mentioned earlier. If you guys are going to be involved in this, even a little bit, I think I owe you one of these."

"Thank you," Chad said and put his in his pocket, "Now, Steve told me about the money raising ideas he had, and those are good. Getting the word out to your supporters is always worthwhile, and a getting them to donate to your cause is always great.

"But what we need first are some nice propaganda victories. Things that are easy to accomplish, which give the other side a black eye, and brings you both acclaim and followers. Easy victories to make you look like a winner, followed up by something a little more difficult to make it clear that you're a serious contender."

"And just what would those things be?" Roxy asked.

"Ah! These things always write themselves," Chad said with a smile, "all I need is good current intel on what the councils you see as your enemies are up to, as well as the ones you see as on the fence, along with all the background you have on them.

"But the first thing you always want to do, is hit them where they think they're strongest. Because this early in the war, they won't be expecting it and the psychological damage to them will be considerable, even if the damage is minimal."

"Like when Doolittle bombed Japan?" Daelyn spoke up.

Chad nodded, "Exactly! So where are each of these councils strongest?"

"At their coven houses," Jolene said. "Where they meet to discuss business, council business, and do any rituals or circle casting."

"And what's the worst thing you can do to their coven house?"

"Burn it down?" Daelyn asked.

Chad shook his head, "Too impersonal." Chad turned to Jolene, "Why do they use the coven house, why not meet at the leader's home?"

"Because they're old and the circle enchantments are steeped in power...." Jolene stopped and smiled at Chad, "and if we were to disrupt the circle, it would take them couple of days to rebuild it."

"And they wouldn't be able to cast? Or circle?"

Jolene shook her head, "No, they'd still be able to do those things, but it would be harder and cost them more power. And once they got it restored, it wouldn't be as powerful or settled as the one we ruined.

"Oh, they'd be annoyed at the very least, possibly even pissed."

"How hard would it be?" Sean asked.

Jolene grinned, "Not very. That's why they keep them in a separate place, to keep them from accidentally being ruined."

"How well guarded are the houses?" Roxy asked.

"As I recall, not very," Jolene said, "but I haven't been to many of them. They do guard them when they're being used fairly well, but when they're not?" Jolene shrugged, "They're not viewed as high value targets to most people."

Chad grinned, "But the rank and file will see it, and they'll look at their leaders and wonder just what is going on and demand answers."

"Won't they just write it off as a harmless prank?" Daelyn said.

"If your enemies broke into your most sacred place and your leaders told you 'it was nothing, just an annoyance,' would you believe them? Or would you think they were hiding something and become suspicious?"

Daelyn shrugged, "Why wouldn't I believe them?"

"Because we're gonna lie about what we did there, that's why!" Chad laughed. "No matter what the leaders say, there's always going to be that small kernel of doubt, and we'll play on that, trust me, we will."

"But why would they believe you? The others in that council group, that is."

"It all depends on just how honest the leaders are with their people. Most leaders aren't very, and from what you've told me about these people already, and their love of secrets, I suspect there will be a lot of suspicion."

Jolene nodded, "He's right, Dae. My uncle's a leader of one of the better covens, and even they get pretty secretive at times. From what I've seen of the ones we've had problems with so far, they're a lot worse."

"So," Sean said, "we do a raid on the coven houses of the councils we're up against, then what?"

"Then you recruit," Chad said.

Sunday Morning

Sean looked out the back window of Daelyn's 'Cuda as they slowly cruised through the graveyard. Mountain View Cemetery was right off the highway, though you couldn't get there directly. They came up five-eighty of course and then just took eighty until the exit just past the place.

Roxy was sitting in the front seat, so she could enjoy Daelyn's driving like a complete maniac on the way up here on the highway. Fortunately, early Sunday mornings in Reno, most of the streets were deserted.

They'd left Jolene back at the bunker to work on some defensive spells and some other odds and ends. The bunker was definitely someplace they were going to stay a while, so they might as well make it as comfortable as possible, as well as making it hard to find and well defended.

"So, where's the center?" Daelyn asked from the front.

"The circle, that's it. Just drive around it slowly, once."

Daelyn did that, and as she did Sean looked around for a big concrete flower planter.

"What about your grandfather's grave?"

"Too obvious," Sean and Roxy said at the same time. Roxy looked back at him and grinned, so he leaned forward and kissed her.

"You two are sickening," Daelyn sighed.

"Oh, once you get over being embarrassed, you'll be sickening too," Roxy chuckled.

"Oh? What about Jo?"

"Jo only does lewd," Roxy snickered.

Daelyn sighed.

"Over there," Sean said pointing to a crypt that was just off one of the side roads that led like spokes from the center road that circled the offices and the wake halls for the cemetery. There were two rather large cement flowerpots right in front of it.

Daelyn nodded and pulled the car to a stop in front of the crypt, Roxy opening the door and quickly getting out as the car stopped. Flipping the seat forward, Sean followed as Daelyn also got out of the car and they walked up to the pots.

"Which one is it?" Daelyn asked.

"No idea," Sean said walking up to the one on the left. "I guess we try one, and if that doesn't work, we try the other."

"Why not try both?" Roxy asked walking up to the other one. "So, what do we have to do?"

"Push down on it then turn it clockwise a quarter turn. Then pull up on it and turn counter-clockwise a quarter turn. After that, you should simply be able to lift it up."

"And it's under the urn?" Daelyn asked.

"Supposedly," Sean said and pressing down on the concrete, he felt something give a little. Turning it was fairly hard, it was stiff and there was sand or something in the mechanism.

"This one's not moving," Roxy grunted.

"Sean's is," Daelyn said.

When he got it the full quarter turn, Sean pulled up on it. It took a lot of strength and he had to strain at it. Once he felt it stop rising, he then had to fight the grinding mechanism again and turn it all the way back, where it stopped.

Sean looked around to see if anyone was watching them.

"Anyone watching?" he asked the girls.

"Not that I can tell, why?"

"Cause I'm gonna have to shift to lift this. This thing is *heavy*."

"We're good."

Bending his knees and lowering himself, Sean quickly shifted and wrapping his arms around it, he slowly stood up, grunting as he did so. He could feel it pulling up out of the ground, but it was even heavier than he had thought.

"Damn, Sampson must have been hella strong to have pulled this out of the ground!" Sean grunted. A moment later, Roxy joined him, helping him to lift it up.

"Okay, I can see under it," Daelyn said, looking down into the deep hole that was now revealed. Recessed off to one side was a square metal lined cubby with a black rectangular bag sitting in it, which the plug of the pot would easily seal. "There's a plastic bag, just a moment!" She said and scrambling around to the other side and reaching down into the hole she grabbed it and pulled it out.

"Got it, now don't drop it! Lower it back into place."

Grunting, Sean quickly put it back down, and then turned it back part way so no one else could easily lift it out. Though easy was probably a relative term!

""Come on, I think we're drawing attention!" Daelyn said and jumped back into the car.

Shifting back, Sean followed Roxy back to the car, diving in the back seat as she slid into the front. Sure enough, looking out the back window he could see someone was trotting over to investigate as Daelyn suddenly took off.

"At least you didn't spin the tires," Sean chuckled.

"Hey, it's a graveyard, I don't wanna be disrespectful if I don't have ta' be!" Daelyn chuckled and tossed the sealed plastic packet back to Sean.

Taking it in his hands, Sean looked at it. It was a very thick and heavy plastic bag alright, about twelve inches by eight by four, sealed all the way around. Feeling it with his hands, it definitely felt like there was a box or something inside. The problem was he couldn't tear it open, it was definitely too tough, and the back seat of the 'Cuda was too small for him to shift.

"Roxy, be a Hon and lend me a claw for a moment?"

Sean held out the bag as Roxy shifted, and flexing out one long claw from her index finger, she dug into the bag, and then slowly cut it open along one side.

"That's pretty tough stuff," Roxy commented.

"It sure is," Sean said and now that he was able to get his hands inside it, he slowly ripped it open the rest of the way. Inside, there was a wooden box, with a latch. Taking the box out of the bag and opening the box he saw that a book sat inside, filling it. Attached to the inside of the lid, there was a small pendant that was about the size and shape of a military dog tag, that looked to be made out of the same material as the lycan chain that he now wore around his neck.

The moment Sean touched it; he felt the power in it. Bring up his enchanting spell he started to check it over as Daelyn drove. Whatever it was, it was complicated. The spell on it was massive, far greater and far more involved than the one on the lycan chain was, and studying it would not be easy, if even possible, as the spell was constantly changing as he looked at it!

That surprised him. Sean had no idea something like that could be done, but he remembered his father's warning about the power that this item contained. It could very well be that his father knew a secret method to keep others from learning his techniques, which considering how jealously alchemists were supposed to have guarded their secrets, only made sense to Sean.

On a hunch, Sean took the tag out and touched it to the bottom of the tiger-eye stone on his necklace. There was a small 'click' and it attached.

"Handy, that," Roxy said, watching him.

"It only makes sense, and it proves my dad made the necklace after all."

"So what is it? What does it do?"

Sean shrugged and looked at the book still sitting in the box. "I have no idea, but I bet it's all inside of this."

"That's great and all," Daelyn started, "but remember about our needing another car?"

"Yeah, I do," Sean told her.

"Well, I see something in that used car lot up ahead, so let's check it out."

Looking around, Sean blinked, "How'd we get over here so ..." he stopped, "Oh yeah, you're driving."

Roxy laughed, "She is fast, isn't she?"

"Considering I usually took the bus, it's going to take some getting used to," Sean agreed.

"So, what are you looking at, that Camaro?" Roxy asked.

"Oh hell no, those things are slow," Daelyn said and pulling into the parking lot she stopped the car and Sean almost laughed as the salesmen just stopped and gawked at Daelyn as she got out. She was wearing a dress again, a rather short one with a nice plunging neckline, as well as those three-inch spike heels.

"Um, may I help you?" the first salesman asked, as Sean climbed out of the back behind Roxy and they circled around the car to join Daelyn.

"Yeah," Daelyn said, "what's the story on that Ram van? Get the keys; I wanna take a look at it."

"Uh, sure," he said tearing his eyes away from Daelyn's chest, "I'll be right back."

"Is that yours?" the other salesman asked Sean, only he was staring at the car instead of Daelyn or Roxy.

"It's hers," Sean said and nodded towards Daelyn.

"Hers?" He said and blinked.

"She rebuilt it," Sean smiled proudly, "I wouldn't even know where to start."

The guy blinked again, looked at Daelyn, then looked at the car, then looked back at Daelyn.

"Would you marry me?" he said.

"Sorry, she belongs to me," Sean laughed and put an arm around Daelyn who was staring at the salesman.

"You'd marry me because I rebuilt a car?"

"No, I'd marry you because you rebuilt a classic muscle car and you're hotter than my ex-wife," the guy laughed then, "why are the good ones always taken? Come on, I'll show you the van while we wait for Chris to find the keys."

Sean just stood back and watched, along with Roxy, as Daelyn gave the van the once over, popping the engine cover off inside the van, and then starting it up. She revved it a couple of times, put the cover back on, then took it out onto the street and up and down the block a few times.

After she was done, she pulled back in and parked it.

"Okay," Daelyn said climbing down out of it. "Two grand."

"What! I can't sell it that cheap!"

Daelyn rolled her eyes, "Look, if you know enough to appreciate what I did for the 'Cuda, you know that third gear is almost shot, the reverse gear synchro is going, and that the seventh cylinder's got a burnt exhaust valve. Twenty-five, cash, or I'll come back in a month and offer you fifteen for it."

The guy just sighed and looked at Sean, "She always this rough?"

Sean laughed, "I know better than to argue with her when it comes to cars," and reaching into his pocket, he grabbed his bankroll, rather happy that they'd hit the bank up on Thursday. "So, deal?"

"Yeah, deal. Let's go inside and do the paperwork."

Sean nodded and followed the guy inside with Daelyn, while Roxy stayed outside to keep an eye on things. Twenty minutes later, Daelyn had a temporary registration and a bill of sale.

"*Hon*," Daelyn said in a rather sweet and seductive voice all of the sudden.

Sean sighed and looked down at her. "How much?"

Daelyn grinned, "How much ya' got?"

Sean pulled out his bankroll; he'd started off with ten.

"Oh! That'll do!" Daelyn laughed and grabbed it, then pulling him down she kissed him. "I gotta pick up a few things; I'll meet you guys back home in a few, okay?"

"Huh?"

"Hey, Rox! Catch!" Daelyn said and tossed Roxy the keys to the 'Cuda. "Scratch it and I'll scratch you!"

Shaking his head he watched as Daelyn almost danced over to the van and climbing up inside it, started it up, and then barreled out of the parking lot at full throttle.

"She's going to Summit Racing, isn't she?" the salesman sighed.

"Are they open Sundays?" Sean asked, going around to the other side of the car as Roxy got into the driver's seat.

"Yup."

"Then I suspect that's the case," Sean got in and closed the door as Roxy started the car. "Can you drive stick?" He asked her.

Roxy laughed and putting the car in gear took off out of the parking lot leaving a fair bit of rubber along the way. "Sheriff's kid, I can drive *anything!*"

"You wreck it, and Daelyn will kill you."

"Pfft, I'm a cheetah, fast things and me get along. Besides, I went through the same driver's school the cops do. Don't worry, I can *drive!*"

Sean just sighed and did his best to refrain from holding on to the seat with a death grip.

Daelyn didn't make it back down into the bunker until three hours later.

"Do you have any of my money left?" Sean sighed, looking up from his father's book that he'd been reviewing heavily since he'd gotten back. There were a lot of very interesting and unique spells in it, and he'd identified three he needed to start with. He just had to pick which of the three to do first.

"I stopped for some groceries and something to drink," Daelyn blushed, "so err, just a couple hundred."

"What'd you get to drink?" Jolene asked.

"Oh, a couple kegs of beer. Nothing fancy."

"Dwarves," Roxy sighed, "gotta love 'em! You pick up a tap too?"

"Of course! What, do you think I'm stupid? Help me get them down here; the fridge is big enough to hold both of them."

Sean just sighed and went back to studying his father's book.

"Did you pick something up other than beer?" Jolene asked as Roxy and Daelyn headed back up the stairs.

"What else is there?"

"Wine!" Jolene called and then sighed.

"Don't look at me, I drink water most of the time," Sean said without looking up. "We couldn't afford soda."

"Well, hopefully it's good beer."

"She's a dwarf; of *course* it's good beer."

Sean went back to the book as the girls wrestled the kegs down the stairs, though to be honest; it wasn't much of a wrestle. Roxy had shifted and was simple holding it over her head, while Daelyn was holding the other one against her chest with her arms wrapped around it, reminding Sean that dwarves, even the women, were pretty damn strong.

Ten minutes later, Daelyn came out of the bedroom wearing her coveralls with a tool case in either hand.

"I'll be upstairs working on the van, if anyone needs me!" Daelyn said rather cheerfully and headed up the stairs.

"Well we won't be seeing her again for a while," Roxy sighed and plopped down next to Sean. "What are you up to?"

"Looking over the spells in my father's book and trying to decide the best place to start."

"Looks complicated."

Sean nodded, "My father was obviously a genius. The things he's got in here are just amazing. I found the spell to enchant the tags, and it definitely is a protection from silver device, but it's not just a spell, it's an incredibly involved system. It'll take me months just to learn everything involved in it, before I can even begin to try and learn the process for making one."

"What about your tarball spell?"

Sean shook his head, "It's got a pretty involved encryption algorithm running over the top of everything. I can't run the tarball spell against it, until I've figured out how to crack that."

"Isn't that in the book?"

Sean nodded, "First section of the book, teaches how it works, how to cast it, how to get past it, all of that."

"Well, I guess that's where you should start," Roxy smiled.

"Yeah, but what's the key?"

"Key?"

"Every encryption programs need a key," Sean told her.

"Well, I'd say to learn the program, err, learn the spell, and find out what kind of key it uses. I'm sure whatever it is, your father probably left you a hint someplace."

Sean nodded, "I guess you're right. Did Daelyn pick up any food while she was out?"

"Yup! Well, you go study while Jo and I go deal with *other* things," Roxy winked and suddenly Jolene didn't look so bored anymore.

"Let me know when you've made dinner," Sean chuckled. "Until then, go have fun."

Sean watched as his women sauntered off to the bedroom. Roxy and Jolene had been lovers before he'd come along. As Sean understood things, it was more a matter of Jolene wanting power and Roxy wanting a good time, at first. Apparently they'd gotten fairly close over the last couple of years, which was why when Roxy and Sean had gotten in trouble; Jolene had been the first person Roxy called.

And of course it hadn't taken Sean long to realize that he wanted Jolene himself, and not much longer for Jolene to realize that she wanted

Sean as well. Though Sean often suspected that his already having Roxy as his woman had sweetened that deal for Jolene.

It was nice to see that they still had feelings for each other, and he wondered just how long it would take Jolene to seduce Daelyn. Jolene was a tantric witch after all, and honestly, it just wasn't about the sex with her, she was an incredibly loving woman and if you actually loved her back it triggered some very deep responses inside her. Sean had a suspicion that there might be something in Jolene's past that had led to that behavior, but right now he had his own problems to deal with.

Digging back into the book, Sean had to agree with Roxy. He needed to learn the encryption spell. Then he needed to learn its key so he could get through the encryption to archive the entire device. It would most likely be a year before he could even start to construct one himself, and then he'd only be able to put out one a year, *if* he used his father's methods.

Using the tarball he could create one in a couple of minutes. However the power requirements would obviously be huge.

Well, he'd tackle that problem when he came to it. There was that entire section on 'energy management,' hopefully he'd find an answer in there.

Sean yawned and leaning back in the seat he closed the book and set it down. Looking around, there was no one in the room, and it was quiet. Looking down he saw the empty beer mug sitting on the seat besides him, and remembered now that Roxy had handed it to him, along with a plate of food....

Sean didn't see the plate, but he vaguely remembered eating. He'd been so heavily wrapped up in the learning the spell that he'd really not been paying attention to anything else around him. He'd taken it apart and put it together in his head a dozen times, going over each aspect as he learned it. It was a thing of beauty and his father really had been paying attention to the things that went on in the real world, having taken the 'family' encryption method that *his* father had passed down to him, and updated it with techniques stolen from the lost keys method.

Cracking the encryption on the tag would be so hard that it might as well be impossible. But Sean at least had an idea of what the key looked like, format wise, so when he found it, he'd hopefully know it.

He tarballed the encryption spell, then used it on the book, locking it to himself with a keyphrase. No one would be able to read what was inside it now, other than him, going forward. The encryption spell alone was something he didn't want anyone getting their hands on, and the description of the functioning of the spell on the 'Silver Tag' as he now thought of it, was something he wasn't ready to share yet.

The device was a protection from silver system alright, but the description at the front of the spell hinted at just how complicated it was.

It started off as a shield spell that covered your body, and only your body. Even your clothing was outside of the effect of the spell, same for your hair or fur if it was long enough. The spell hovered literally on the surface of your skin, to conserve energy, as it was always armed and ready to go.

The second silver hit it; the spell immediately went into action by splitting an alpha particle off of every silver atom, turning it into a rhodium atom. The energy from the release of the alpha particle was captured by the spell and used to power the spell's functions, of which there were several.

Most of the power that was captured was used to corral the electrons freed when the alpha particle was split off, to pair those electrons back to the alpha particle and turn it into helium-four, a stable element, to cut down on radiation given off by the shield.

But that wasn't the really brilliant part; for all that it was brilliant to start with. While only about ten percent of the power was left over from that function for the device to use, when you considered just how many silver atoms there were in a silver bullet, that power added up phenomenally fast. That power was used to harden the shield and increase its power. The processes of transmuting the silver slowed the silver coming through the shield down, as it generated a kinetic force due to simple physics. So as the power of the shield increased, that kinetic response also grew and started to repel any silver coming in contact with it, with greater and greater force, and eventually *any* metallic object! Until it reached a point where the shield would simply rebound any metal thrown against it in an inelastic manner, deforming or shattering the bullet.

The next stage would be that the shield would begin to expand, slowly, until it was an inch away from the surface of the skin, so it could begin to radiate excess energy as heat, without hurting the person inside the shield, while recharging the magical energies of the lycan using the device, as it was assumed that the now transformed bullets, or other weapon, would have done the wearer some damage in the initial attack.

That last statement lead Sean into calling up his own 'character sheet' and doing some extensive examinations of his own abilities. He was able to confirm what he'd been told earlier: that it wasn't just shifting that used a lycan's magical energy, but their regeneration abilities sucked it down as well. Which was why lycans had so much energy.

And why he suspected now so few of them were magic users. As a magic user, if he cast too much of his power, he would not only be unable to shift, but he'd be unable to regenerate as well!

Sean stopped and thought about that a moment, happy that he'd discovered *that* little pitfall here in his father's book, rather than out in a fight, where it might kill him. He also realized where that extra bit of energy he was having trouble accounting for was coming from when he ran his tarball spell. He was also doing a version of alpha decay on those items! He'd have to learn how to use his father's spell for canceling the radiation output, or he was liable to harm himself, or one of the girls!

Going over to the refrigerator, he drew a fresh mug of beer and quickly drank it down. Checking his watch, he saw that it was after three in the morning.

Getting another mug, he took a few drinks from it, and decided to go upstairs to their little garage and see what Daelyn had managed to do so far. After sitting on that concrete seat, for the last twelve hours, cushions or not, he definitely needed to stretch his legs.

Going upstairs the Dodge Ram van looked like it had undergone some sort of explosion, however a fairly orderly one. There were parts laid out everywhere, and the old engine had apparently been replaced by a newer and much larger looking one. There were also what looked like suspension pieces and parts everywhere.

Sean found Daelyn sound asleep, lying on a mechanic's creeper under the transmission that was also in a good many parts, none of which he could make head nor trails of.

Rolling the creeper out, he first pulled off her gloves, then started to undo her coveralls.

"Huh? What?" Daelyn said rather groggily as Sean leaned down and kissed her. Other than some grease and oil smears on her face and in her hair, she was actually fairly clean. Though her coveralls were a filthy mess.

"Bed time," Sean whispered and with his right hand pulled the coveralls down past that nice little ass of hers while pulling her against him with his left.

"I gotta work on the car," Daelyn yawned.

"You were sleeping, there is a better place for that," Sean chuckled and standing up, he pressed her against the wall and kissed her again.

"And that place is?" Daelyn gasped as he moved down her body, kissing her neck.

"My bed of course," Sean purred and started in on that lovely chest of hers.

Daelyn sighed as Sean made love to her, with her pressed up against the wall. While the concrete may have been cold, his body was definitely very warm, and his hands and mouth were very talented as he worked his way down her body. She'd grown up around strong men, dwarves were all by their nature incredibly strong for their size, but she'd noticed that Sean really wasn't quite conscious of his. She might be small, but Daelyn was by no means light, considering the amount of muscle on her frame, and even dwarven bones were made of denser and heavier materials than human ones.

Yet he still treated her like she weighted nothing at all to him.

When he finally brought her to a rather satisfying completion, he moved up her body and having shucked his own pants, he entered her tight warmth and drove her to complete distraction a second time. Wrapping her legs around his hips and her arms around his neck, she saw the same look in his eyes that he often turned on Roxy and Jolene. She could see the lion lurking in the background, he may have only been transformed a few weeks ago, but Daelyn could see that Sean had taken well to his lion side. He didn't even question how he could take three women as his mates, or that he could love them all.

He simply did it. Not unlike he was now doing her and the words of love and tenderness coming from his lips were obviously sincere. Dwarves had a gift for telling when someone's words were true, or when they were lies, it came from generations of bartering and dealing with the other races, some of which could be quite glib and deceiving. But Sean wasn't, not with her, not at all. Daelyn's uncle had been honest with her; when he told her Sean was the best deal she'd ever get in a husband.

And her aunt had been equally right when she'd told her that lions were known for their passions and their commitment. That it would be strange at first, but she would love him in the end.

To be honest, Daelyn suspected she was there already, when it came to the loving part. He definitely made her feel like no one before ever had, and that wasn't even taking the sex into account!

They hit their peaks together, and Daelyn clung to Sean as he held her close, the two of them savoring the moment.

"I'd swear that you're just trying to get me pregnant," Daelyn sighed.

Sean laughed, "I think I have to bite you first for that. Hey, can dwarves become lycans?"

Daelyn leaned her head forward to rest it on his shoulder, against the crook of his neck.

"No, and no," she replied.

"Huh?" Sean said, confused.

"Dwarves can't become lycans. And you don't have to turn me into one just to get me pregnant."

Sean took a step back from the wall, sliding one hand up Daelyn's sweaty back to keep her close, not that he suspected she was going anywhere with the grip she had on him.

"I can get you pregnant?"

"Ummhmm," she almost laughed at the surprise in his voice. Obviously there were still things he was learning. "Though you don't have to worry about it just yet."

"But," Sean looked down at her confused, while the sight of her clinging to him definitely did things for his ego, and other parts as well.

"But I thought lycans could only breed lycans?"

"Didn't my mother mention to you that lions are the exception to the rules?"

"Well, yeah, but I didn't realize she meant," Sean stopped a moment, "So I can get Jo pregnant?"

"You can get damn near any female pregnant." Daelyn yawned, "Now, how about bed?"

Sean nodded and started for the stairs, he suspected that by the time he got to the bottom of them, he'd ready for another round. If Daelyn didn't fall asleep on him at least. But this was definitely something to think about.

"So, you'd have little werelions?"

"No, I'd have dwarves. A lion's offspring are whatever the mother's race is."

"Huh."

"MmmHmm. Now bed. I want something warm and soft under me this time."

"We'll wake the others," Sean warned.

"That's your problem," Daelyn giggled, "cause I'm sure I'll be long asleep before you're done with them.

The Shot Heard Around the World

Sean sat in the van as they pulled up to the coven house for the Council of Ascendance. This was the last one on the list that they'd spent all day Monday going over. All of the major councils got a visit, but after talking it over with Chad they decided not to antagonize the ones that had so far been *not* been hostile. Erudito, Sapientia, and Vestibulum had each gotten a card left in the middle of their circle, telling them that their world was about to change, and that their help would make it a peaceful and orderly transition.

Sean had signed each of those cards.

Totis Viribus, and The Tall Men, who had been involved in the storm as well as attacks on Sean, had their circles destroyed, the only calling card had been a single lion's footprint, that Sean had made, using a stamp they'd found in a store.

At the coven house for the council of Gradatim, which they'd just left, Sean had also left the same mark, after they'd destroyed their circle.

At the Sorceress's guild, Chad had suggested that they leave a sympathy card for those who had died from Totis's treachery, one telling them that if they didn't take sides, they'd be left alone.

Sean hadn't been sure that that was a great idea, but Chad said the unspoken point was those opposing Sean were not to be trusted and their allies would be betrayed.

"Last one," Sean sighed, looking around. Daelyn had spent yesterday putting a huge vinyl stickers on both sides of the van that proclaimed them to be exterminators. Sean hadn't asked where she'd gotten them from, as he really didn't want to know. She'd finished with the van on Monday, they'd then spent Tuesday driving around checking their targets and going over just how to destroy a circle as quickly as possible.

Climbing out of the van in their white paper coveralls with the logo of the exterminating company on the back, they walked up to the door, and while Roxy kept watch, Sean quickly sprung it using a flat bar.

Stepping inside, they both shifted and using their enhanced senses, listened carefully.

"All clear," Roxy said, and Sean nodded.

Making their way into the building they started a quick search, circles had to be in contact with the ground, either drawn in dirt, or on rock, or even concrete set into the ground, if it was prepared properly. The building they were in was on a foundation, so either there was a room that stepped down, or a basement. In either case, they started looking for it immediately.

What they found was the same as the others, a large room in the center of the building with no windows, other than a circular skylight above. The only difference was the flooring. Ascendance had a floor made of poured concrete; the others had used either mortared stone, or in the case of Gradatim, brick.

Moving to opposite sides of the circle, Sean took out a hammer and his flat bar and started to chisel though one of the lines of the crucible as Roxy did the same on the other side. It took a little longer than he thought it would, the concrete was fairly tough, but a minute later and he was done. Putting his tools away he reached for his stamp when someone kicked in the door and started shooting.

The second shot hit Roxy, who screamed and jumped up in the air, shocking the hell out of Sean. Without even thinking he dashed forward at the man with the gun who was now shooting at him.

As Sean closed the distance he suddenly realized that he recognized the man, and that he only had one arm!

"I'll kill you just like I killed your friend!" The guy screamed at Sean, still pulling the trigger one more time as Sean finally grabbed the man's hand, crushing it around the pistol.

Roxy was keening now behind him; he could see her lying on the floor in a heap out of the corner of his eye as he pulled the man closer and grabbed him by the throat.

"Why aren't you dying! Those bullets..." were the last words the man got out as Sean sunk his claws into the man's neck and ripped out his throat, blood spraying everywhere.

Letting go of him, Sean turned and ran back to Roxy, and sweeping her up into his arms he ran out of the building. Two other people were between him and the door, and both were armed. Wrapping his arms around Roxy, he shifted her to the side and twisted his body, leading with his left shoulder as they shot at him to keep her out of the line of fire.

Sean could feel the shield taking in energy, they were using silver bullets!

Smashing into the first one, they went flying into a wall and slid down it in a shocked daze as the second one's pistol ran out of bullets. They just stared at Sean in shock as Sean plowed past them next, using his tail to knock them over as he just smashed into the door and ran through it.

Jolene had the side door to the van open and Sean just dove into the back of the van as Daelyn took off like a shot, Jolene slamming the door closed behind them.

"What happened?" Jolene asked, looking down at Sean who was covered in blood, and Roxy who was gasping and keening softly.

"Silver bullets," Sean growled and ripping off Roxy's coverall he found the wound, she'd been shot in the gut, and the bullet hadn't come out the other side.

"What do I do?" Sean asked, looking up at Jolene, whose face had gone ash white.

"The... there's nothing, nothing you can do," Jolene gasped.

Roxy grabbed onto Sean's arm, squeezing it tightly as she keened loudly in obvious pain.

"What do you mean there's nothing we can do?" Sean growled loudly as the van plowed around a corner, throwing them all against the side and making Roxy keen louder.

"It's silver; it's gotta be in her blood by now! Maybe if the bullet had gone clean through, but it didn't, it's slowly killing her, an inch at a time. It's like a poison, there's no way you can get it all out now."

Sean looked down at her. Roxy, *his* Roxy! He wanted to scream, he wanted to roar, and right now he wanted to go back there and kill them all.

"Are you alright?"

"Huh?" Sean looked up at Jolene, she was yelling at him.

"Are you alright? Did they shoot you too?"

Sean nodded slowly, "Yeah, I'm alright, the pendant worked. It turned the silver into something else, they couldn't ..."

Sean grabbed the pendant on his collar and pulled on it, with a 'click' it came free.

"What are you doing?" Jolene asked.

"Hoping for a miracle," Sean said and put the tag to the tiger-eye Roxy's collar. Nothing happened.

"Shit! Why won't it attach?"

"Maybe she needs to do it?" Jolene yelled.

"But she's barely conscious," Sean growled.

"Use her fingers to hold it, then try."

Sean nodded and peeling Roxy's fingers off of his arm, he put the tag between her fingers, and squeezing her hand closed with his, he moved the tag end over to the tiger-eye. There was a loud click as it attached.

"I..." Sean started, but Roxy suddenly screamed out loud, arching her back as her eyes came wide open.

"What's happening?" Daelyn yelled form the front seat.

"I don't know!" Sean growled back and grabbing Roxy's shoulders he tried to use his monitoring program on her.

"Jolene, what's wrong?"

"She's out of magic! Her regeneration used it all up fighting the silver and now it's trying to use her life force to heal her!"

"Well feed her power!"

"I'm trying!"

Grabbing Roxy, Sean pulled her close and kissed her, hard, trying to will his energy into her, as her arms grabbed at him, her claws sinking into him. What to do! He couldn't think of what to do! He'd stopped the silver, but she was still dying on him!"

"Can't you heal her?" He heard Daelyn yell from the front seat.

"I'm trying to power her regeneration!" Jolene yelled back.

"Damn, I'm a fool!" Sean muttered and with a gesture he brought up his healing framework and started casting healing spells into Roxy. He went through every spell he had, ones to cure major wounds, ones to repair internal organs, one to restore blood, one to stop poisons, another one for major wounds. His mana level was high, he'd barely cast anything, but right now he was casting everything and anything at all he could think of.

Suddenly Roxy shuddered and went limp in his arms.

"Is, is she...?" Sean gasped looking down at Roxy's now limp body.

"I don't think," Jolene stopped and put her hand on Roxy's chest. "She's alive, she's unconscious, but she's alive."

Sean flopped back against the inside wall of the van, "Thank god," he sighed, suddenly feeling quite drained himself.

"Well, at least we know that the amulet works," Daelyn said shutting off the van.

"We safe?" Sean asked.

"Yeah, I lost the one person who tried to follow us pretty quickly. But the gunshots had drawn the police, so that took a little longer to deal with.

"Great, now the cops are after us!"

"Actually, they're after an exterminator's van. Once I peel off the vinyl and do a little painting, they won't recognize us at all."

Sean nodded, leaning forward he took Jolene's head between his paws and kissed her slowly.

"Thank you for saving Roxy, I love you."

Jolene blushed, "Well, I love her too, and yeah, I even love you, Sean. Just, please don't do this to me or her, or any of us, again?"

Sean sighed, "I wish I could promise that." Turning to look at Daelyn he smiled, "And thank you for getting us out of there, and yes, I love you too."

"Will Roxy be okay?" Daelyn asked in a worried voice.

"I hope so," Sean said, equally worried. He looked up at Jolene, "Jo?"

Jolene sighed, "I don't know. Lycans and silver isn't my strong suit. I could see that the spells you were casting were helping, they helped a lot! And I was able to feed enough power into her that her regeneration stopped trying to feed on her life force. I *think* she'll recover, but what we really need is a healer, an experienced one. Who can look at her and fix anything that we may have missed."

Sean nodded and looked at Daelyn. "Know anybody?"

Daelyn shook her head, "Maybe, but I'm sure my uncle does. I'll need to make some phone calls."

Sean nodded and turning he opened the door, the getting out carefully, he reached back inside and picking up Roxy, he carried her downstairs and put her in their bed.

"I think you're still bleeding," Jolene observed as he put Roxy gently down. He had thought about taking her to the bathroom first and washing all of the blood off, but he worried that she might not be up for being moved around that much.

"Really?" Sean stopped and stepping back he peeled out of the jumpsuit, which due to the collar was extra large now, seeing as he was still in his hybrid form. Looking down at himself, there was a hole in his leg, which was slowly oozing blood.

"I used all of my magic on Roxy," Sean sighed. "I guess I better bandage this up until I gain enough back for my regeneration to work." Sean stopped for a moment, "How come my regeneration isn't trying to suck up my life force?"

Jolene came over and put her hands on him, and closed her eyes a moment.

"You're actually pretty close to it," she told him, "but you're still just barely on the positive side, so your body is healing at the rate that your magic is restoring. I guess it doesn't become an issue until you use up all of your natural magic?"

Sean shrugged, "I don't know. You should clean up, you look like a butcher."

"You first," Jolene laughed nervously, "*you* look like an axe murderer!"

Nodding, Sean took a last look at Roxy and then went into the shower and quickly got all of the blood and gore out of his fur and his mane. By the time he had finished, the wound in his thigh had healed.

Spelling Jolene at Roxy's side, he just held her hand and sat there, until Daelyn came back, almost dragging a much shorter and much much older female dwarf with her.

"Daelyn tells me your mate there was shot with silver?"

Sean nodded.

"And that you got rid of all the silver, is that right?"

Sean nodded again.

"Huh, ain't never heard of that before. Usually a lycan gets shot with silver, that's it, they're dead. So what happened next?"

"I used all of my magic healing her, and my other wife pumped her full of energy. Her regeneration was trying to heal her using her life force."

"Huh, well let me take a look at her," The older dwarf turned to Daelyn, "I'm gonna need a hose, a funnel, and you need to find all the high fat and protein food you got and grind it up into a paste. Thin it with beer. You got beer, right?"

"Yes grandmother!" Daelyn took off like a shot.

"You know what's wrong with her?" Sean said, eyes wide with hope.

"I suspect, now move over and let me take a look. Ya' see, you lycans use a lot of energy, and you get most of it from food. You eat like us dwarves do, part of why yer always welcome at our tables, ya got you some regular appetites."

Sean watched as she took out a number of things that he didn't recognize, and several that he did, like a stethoscope, blood pressure cuff, and an electronic thermometer.

"Anyways, her body is probably kinda deadlocked right now, can't heal anymore cause she needs food, but isn't hurt so badly that it's eating itself.

"Course, if that's the case, it won't last. Which is why we need to start getting food into her."

Sean just nodded and watched as she examined Roxy. Daelyn came in with a plastic tube attached to a blue funnel that Sean suspected she used for changing oil, but it was clean, so he didn't say anything. She also left a pitcher of beer and disappeared again.

"Yup, just as I thought," the old dwarf said. "How'd you get the silver out?"

"My father's device, the one they killed him for," Sean said. "It works."

"Well glory to the earth and stone for that! Now come over here and hold her muzzle open for me, Son, while I get this tube down into her stomach."

Sean nodded and did as he was told, watching as the old woman exhibited a fair amount of skill getting the tube all the way down Roxy's throat until only the blue funnel was in her muzzle.

"How do you know it's not in her lungs?" he asked.

"No air coming out of it," she chuckled. "Now, let's start off with some beer, make sure that I got this right."

Sean watched as she slowly poured a little bit of beer down the funnel, then stopped and checked Roxy's breathing. Then a bit more, again and again, until it was all gone.

"Get me some more beer and light a fire under my granddaughter, will ya?"

Sean ran out of the room and found Daelyn using a pair of knives as she was dicing up everything she could find he guessed.

"Sweep that up into a pitcher and let's go," Sean told her as he filled the one he had back up.

Daelyn nodded and started doing just that as he returned.

The old dwarf had her hand on Roxy's stomach, kneading it slowly.

"What are you doing?" Sean asked, curious.

"Making sure that what's in her stomach doesn't stay there, we got a lot more stuff to put in it." Just then Daelyn came in and handed a pitcher that looked almost like mud to her.

"Ah, good!" She said and started to slowly pour that into the funnel.

"What's in that?" Sean said, wrinkling his nose at the scent.

"Protein bars, raw meat, sugar, chocolate, cream cheese, lard. Whatever I could grab."

Just then Jolene came into the room, munching on a protein bar as well, and handed another one to Sean whose own stomach was growling.

"How long will this take, Grandmother Robin?" Daelyn asked.

"Until her stomach is full. Or she wakes up. Don't go too far, Son. If she comes too suddenly, she ain't gonna be too pleased with having this here funnel and tube down her throat."

Sean nodded and looked longingly at Jolene's protein bar.

"I'll go get you some food," Jolene said with a smile and left.

Thirty minutes later, Grandmother Robin pronounced Roxy 'full' and removed the funnel and tube.

"When will she come to?" Sean asked, quietly.

"Not really sure, Son. She's sleeping now; her body is pretty much concentrated on digesting everything we gave her. Plus she went through a pretty traumatic experience. Silver has a pretty nasty effect on lycans. She may wake up in an hour, may not until tomorrow."

Sean nodded, "Thank you. I owe you a lot for your help."

Grandmother Robin chuckled, "Ya married my granddaughter, which makes you family. Think nothin' of it."

Sean nodded, "I'm grateful all the same."

"And you're welcome. Now, Daelyn, take me home and see if maybe you can keep that monster machine of yours south of the speed limit for a change!"

Sean smiled at Daelyn as she led her grandmother out of the room.

"Now what?" Jolene asked.

"I think I should call her father, and let him know she's alright."

Jolene nodded. "I'll sit here and keep an eye on her."

"Thanks, Love," Sean kissed her on the forehead and then went out into the kitchen and found his pants. Shifting back to his human form, now that he had enough power back to do so, he put them on, and getting out his phone he went upstairs and then out of the garage and into the darkness. John had told him that the only way they could track his phone now would be to try and triangulate off of the towers he was picked up by. As long as he didn't use it in the same place twice they'd never figure out where he was, assuming that they even thought to try that. Usually they just went for the GPS information on your phone.

Putting the battery in, he turned it on. He would have used the burner phone, but he had no idea what Roxy's father's number was, but it was stored in his phone.

He was still sorting through the directory list when the phone rang. Looking at it in surprise, he saw it was Roxy's father.

"Hello," Sean sighed.

"About time you turned your damn phone on!" Sean heard Mr. Channing growl. "How's my daughter? She had damn well better be fine!"

"She's fine," Sean sighed.

"Then put her on!"

"She's still sleeping."

"The rumor is she was attacked, with silver! What the hell happened?"

"We were surprised by one of the Ascendance members while leaving them a little love letter in their coven hall," Sean sighed.

"What! Are you crazy?"

"Obviously. Anyway, we got surprised by a one-armed man who I recognized. He shot Roxy first, then he shot me a bunch."

"Wait, was he using silver bullets?"

"Yup."

"So why aren't you dead?"

"Why do you think?" Sean grumbled. "Once I got Roxy out of there, I got rid of the silver in her body, but it had done a lot of damage. Healing that wasn't easy, but we did it. Now she's resting."

"I want to meet with you."

"So do a lot of people," Sean sighed again, "I'll think about it."

"Son, who do you think you're talking with here?"

"A neutral party. One who probably needs to stay neutral. I meet with you; you're probably going to get in trouble and I don't think I want that on my conscience right now. However, I will tell you one thing I learned today."

"What's that?"

"The Ascendance started this whole thing, not the Lithos. They were the ones driving the van that tried to kidnap me."

Bill Channing paused a moment, then asked, "You sure about that?"

"The one-armed man who surprised us? They got his other arm in evidence down at the police station from what happened in the van they tried to kidnap me with."

"Well," Bill Channing said after thinking a minute about what Sean had just told him. "That changes things. You take good care of my daughter. And if this happens again, you and me are gonna have words, Son."

"Bye, Dad." Sean sighed and hung up.

Taking a look at his screen there were a bunch of text messages, they were all from his friends, who he'd since talked to, so he cleared those.

There were also a bunch of messages left on the answering system. So he called that up and let them play.

The first three were from detective Schumer, he deleted those immediately, he really didn't care what Schumer had to say right now.

There was one from his lawyer, about the bike.

Two from Steven, before Sean had caught up with him.

The last one, that stopped him cold.

"Hello, Sean? It's Mom. I, I wanted to wish you a happy birthday. I know the odds of getting you on the phone now are pretty slim, but I don't know of how else to contact you.

"I can't tell you where I am; only that I'm safe, and I'm far away now. Sampson, he saw what was coming and got me out of work, and gave me his car before going after you.

"There's a lot I wish I could have told you, you probably know that by now, if you're still alive. But the deal was if I didn't, you'd be allowed to grow up and live your life as a normal man. Obviously they lied and broke that deal," his mother's voice got rather harsh as she said that.

"Your father was a good man, a great man, I loved him very much. Not being able to tell you about the wonderful things that he did, that was hard. But I did it all for you son. He always told me that you were our future, our brave new world."

Sean heard her gasp a moment.

"Remember that, my Son, my Sean; you are our brave new world. And please, if you can, let me know that you're alive."

Sean waited until the message was done, then deleted it. Going into his message box he played his greeting, it was simply 'This is Sean, leave a message.' Hitting record he spoke into his phone, "You've reached Sean Valens, and I'm very much alive." then pressing the button he saved it.

Checked to be sure it worked, then turned off his phone and pulled the battery back out.

Putting it all in his pocket he sat there a moment and thought about what he'd just heard. His mother was alive! And she'd called him! On his birthday no less! She was safe, and she was far away. Well, at least he knew now what had happened to Sampson's car.

Getting up he went back inside, Daelyn would be back soon, he was sure. He needed to check on Roxy, and he needed to sit down and figure out just how to tarball that damn system, because he needed to make another one, and he needed to make it soon.

Meanwhile

Arthur Troy looked around the table, the heads of the four other main councils were here, and even old Harrison from Eruditio had shown up.

Morgan, the leader of Vestibulum raised his hand to get everyone's attention.

"Gentlemen, I have called this meeting at the request of the leaders of both the Council of Ascendance, and the Council of Gradatim," Arthur noticed that Morgan's voice only mildly showed any of the disdain he had for the two groups. "To discuss today's unexpected events."

"Events!" Harkins thundered, "We were attacked! One of my men was murdered! In our very own coven house! Shot dead by that vicious murdering scum Valens! He came right into our home! Our house! And he killed my right hand man! Our associates at Totis Viribus tells me that they were attacked as well! Only luck saved them from losing any of their coven members to these murderous butchers!"

"Yes!" McConnell thundered then, almost on cue. Arthur wondered if the outrage on the man's face was real, or put on just for the meeting, "They came into our coven house as well! They destroyed our circle! A circle that has been sixty years in the making! And then left their foul sign behind after they had left!"

"Gentlemen, please," Morgan sighed, "All of us were visited by Mr. Valens, or perhaps his associates today."

"Oh? Did they destroy your coven circles? Did they damage your homes?"

"Actually," Morgan smiled, "he left us a simple message. As I understand he did at both of your coven houses, Troy, Harrison?"

Troy and Harrison both nodded.

"And just what did this missive they left say?" Harkins asked angrily.

"It was a warning from Mr. Valens that our world was about to change, and a request for our help in making it a peaceful and orderly transition."

"And just what is that supposed to mean!"

"It means," old Harrison sighed from his seat at the table, "that young Sean has taken on the mantle of his father. He means to free the lycans from those of you who still keep them against their own wills and better interests."

"So," McConnell said, "it's a threat!"

"To you, perhaps," Harrison said, nodding slowly. "To me it is just the inevitable finally coming to pass."

"You would side with him?" McConnell glared, his flabby neck and thin face making him look more humorous than dangerous, Arthur felt.

"We side with no one, Roger. Put it back in your pants. I'm simply stating the facts as they are. When you moved against Ben Valens, I warned you all that this would come around again, and now it has."

"And what of you, Troy?" Harkins asked, glaring over at Arthur. "Where do you stand? I've heard that your round-heeled niece has taken up with the Valens' boy!"

"Yes, I believe she has. I even had a few words with him last week, which I am sure most, if not all of you, know about at this point?" Arthur said with a smile.

"And he didn't attack you?" Morgan asked.

Arthur shook his head, "No, but I did manage to upset him, I fear I have misjudged him."

"How so?"

"The young man is already an accomplished mage. I suspect an accomplished alchemist like his father, as well."

"Wait, what?!" Harkins leaned forward in his chair, hands on the table before him. "That's impossible, we had him geased! There's no way he could have learned magic!"

"Well, perhaps the geas dissolved when you broke the agreement?"

"What! How dare you say that! We of the Council of Ascendance have always kept our word! We had nothing to do with the attacks on the Valens' boy! Everyone here knows that!"

Arthur raised an eyebrow, "Oh? Is that so? Tell me, your *right hand* man, just what was his right arm doing in the van that attempted to kidnap the Valens' boy?"

"What! How dare you accuse us of breaking our vow!"

Arthur shrugged, "I have it on good authority that Valens killed your man because he was one of the ones who kidnapped him, and the one that killed his warden and mentor, Sampson. Deny it all you wish, it will not," Arthur smiled slowly, "change the facts."

"And just how did you learn this?"

"I have my sources."

"Harkins, sit down!" Morgan growled, and then turned to Arthur, "Troy, you say he's become powerful?"

Arthur nodded, "No one has been able to scry him for how long now? And when I cast two powerful spells on him, one of paralyzation and another of sleep, they had no effect at all."

"Perhaps your niece?"

Arthur shook his head, "I know my niece's abilities, the Valens' boy has learned and mastered much in a very short time. I can only surmise that his father prepared for this day."

"What of his mother?" Morgan pressed, "I know he believes we had her kidnapped, or," Morgan glanced at Harkins and McConnell, "killed."

"As far as I know, she is no longer here. Whether she left, or was murdered like Sampson, I don't know. Neither apparently, does anyone else.

"However, allow me to point out that the geas placed on her is most likely broken now as well, with the breaking of faith by the Council of Ascendance."

"Take that back!" Harkins yelled, raising to his feet and pointing at Arthur.

"Or what? You'll have your men raise another storm and try to kill me?" Arthur laughed, "You have no idea yet what you've wrought, what you've brought down on all of our heads. Ben Valens was a kind man, the sort of man who saw the good in everyone and always tempered his response in all things.

"Sean Valens? He's a mean son-of-a-bitch with an axe to grind and you just gave him every reason in the world to hate and mistrust us."

Arthur stood, "With the breaking of faith by the Council of Ascendance, the Council of Sapientia withdraws from this conclave. We do not traffic with oathbreakers."

"Take that back!" Harkins yelled again.

"I'll leave you all with one last thought," Arthur said as he headed for the door.

"And that is?" Morgan asked.

"The silver bullets fired at Sean Valens, who as we all now know a lion-were, did not affect him, nor did they kill the female lycan who was with him."

"What! Impossible! I was told he carried her out of there!" Harkins yelled as Arthur left the room, and let the door close behind him.

"Well, that could have gone better, right Arthur?"

Arthur sighed and shook his head as the two men of his bodyguard detail formed up on either side. Currently there was an opening for the number three position.

"I fear not, Dean. The only positive thing that has happened today was Sean didn't destroy Vestibulum's circle as well, and I think Morgan knows that."

"But they didn't try to kill the kid."

"Yes, but they did try to kidnap him, and none of us are naive enough to believe they would have let him live, at least not as anything less than a slave. The young man is showing restraint. He's picked his targets, and now he's isolating them from the rest of us. I have no doubt that Morgan will take a wait and see stance, just like we are, and both Harkins and McConnell, and their people will be hung out to dry."

"Still, he's just one kid, and a couple of girls," James, his other guard said with a shrug.

Arthur sighed and shook his head. He'd heard the rumors of a sudden influx of lycan necklaces on the market. Then there was what happened today, Harkins' people had been quick to blab to everyone and anyone that they'd shot a lycan, a *lion* lycan, a dozen times with silver bullets, *and nothing had happened.* Arthur kept up with lycan customs, beliefs and even their superstitions, to lycans, lions were special. They were also rare.

And now Sean not only was one, but one with a gift to deliver those still in bondage, out of it. A messiah figure if there ever was one.

Arthur had gone over the reports that James had brought him on Sean. The young man had done well enough in public school to earn a scholarship to college, all while working nearly every afternoon and weekend at low paying and often low-status jobs. This was a young man who understood sacrifice and determination, and wasn't afraid to do what had to be done to survive.

"Slave revolts are an ugly thing, James," Arthur said as he got into his car.

"Yeah, but don't they always lose?"

"Most times, yes, but you know who else always loses as well?"

"No, Boss, I don't."

"Slave *owners.*"

End Book Two

Afterword

Hi! I'd like to thank you for reading my story: Perfect Strangers. I hope you enjoyed it, and if you did I would greatly appreciate it if you would rate and review it on Amazon. We do get rewarded by Amazon, when we get four and five star reviews, and of course, the more we get, the more we get rewarded.

What is that reward you ask? Simple: Amazon will show my book to people who they think will enjoy it, like you did.

So please! I'd appreciate it very much if you gave me a good review.

If you find any typo's or 'wrong words' please feel free to email what and where they were to me. Typo's *always* make it through, no matter how many people I have checking things.

Oh! And that Cashier at McDonalds? He's fine! He was just knocked unconscious for a minute.

If you'd like to read more about the continuing trials of Sean, as he tries to find his way through this new world he's been dropped into the middle of while trying to continue his father's work (with the help of course of Roxy, Jolene, and Daelyn), please buy the next book in the series when it comes out!

Book three: Over Our Heads
Book four: Head Down
Book five: When It Falls

(Later books in this series have not yet been titled, though the plots have been developed)

Other stories of mine already out: Shadow, which can be found, along with this on Amazon, by going to my Amazon Author's webpage at:
https://www.amazon.com/Jan-Stryvant/e/B06ZY7L62L/
Or my own webpage at:
www.vanstry.net/stryvant/
Occasional announcements at:
https://stryvant.blogspot.com/